SEA OF LOVE

When she is left destitute, Ellen Campbell embarks on a new life in Australia, a dangerous voyage into the unknown, to marry James, a man she has never met. Helping to nurse a sick passenger, Ellen meets and falls in love with Richard Gray, the ship's doctor. Convinced that he does not return her feelings, she dreads reaching Sydney and having to decide whether to honour her promise to James or face life alone in a strange country.

Books by Roberta Grieve
in the Linford Romance Library:

A HATFUL OF DREAMS
THE COMFORT OF STRANGERS
THE CROSS AND THE FLAME

8|10

R   2017

T

8

10p

1 0 NOV 2023

ROBERTA GRIEVE

SEA OF LOVE

Complete and Unabridged

LINFORD
Leicester

First published in Great Britain in 2008

First Linford Edition
published 2009

British Library CIP Data

Grieve, Roberta
    Sea of love.—Large print ed.—
Linford romance library
    1. Love stories
    2. Large type books
    I. Title
    823.9′2 [F]

    ISBN 978–1–84782–603–9

Published by
F. A. Thorpe (Publishing)
Anstey, Leicestershire

Set by Words & Graphics Ltd.
Anstey, Leicestershire
Printed and bound in Great Britain by
T. J. International Ltd., Padstow, Cornwall

This book is printed on acid-free paper

1

Purple clouds raced across the sky, vying with the speed of the waves which crashed with increasing frequency across the bow of the *Caroline*. Ellen Campbell clung to the rail, torn between terror and exhilaration, careless of the wind which tore at her bonnet, whipping strands of dark wavy hair across her face.

Struggling to survive in the pokey back street tenement in London, she had never dreamed of having such an adventure. That was what it was — an adventure, she told herself. She had to think of it that way, and not as the terrifying ordeal it was turning out to be.

'Get below, get below.'

The shouts of the sailors penetrated the keening of the wind but, despite the danger, Ellen was reluctant to tear herself away from the awesome sight of the spume-laden waves. Remaining on deck seemed preferable to the enforced confinement below decks while the ship fought the storm.

Last time they had battened down the hatches it had been ten days before they saw the sky again — ten days of almost total darkness, clinging to her bunk, listening to the screams and curses of her fellow steerage passengers and inhaling the stench of sickness and fear.

A hand grabbed her arm and a voice screamed in her ear above the roaring of the wind and the snapping of the sails. 'Didn't you hear the order? It's not safe on deck. You must get below.'

She turned and saw that it was not one of the rough sailors but the ship's surgeon. Unlike the other ship's officers he did not seem disdainful of the steerage passengers in their cramped quarters below decks, treating them all with equal courtesy and consideration, especially when they were ill.

Like herself, he seemed to enjoy leaning on the rail and watching the changing seas as the *Caroline* raced towards Australia. In the early days of the voyage they had occasionally exchanged civil greetings, remarking on the blue skies, the balmy weather as the ship scudded along, exclaiming at the sight of flying fish.

She had begun to look forward to their encounters. But one day, as she was laughing with Joan and Millie and a group of the other women from steerage, he had ignored her, taking the arm of the young woman by his side and hustling her into the cabin area below the poop. He obviously regretted his earlier friendliness.

She had last seen him a few days ago when he had seemed to be arguing with the ship's captain. He had turned away abruptly and clattered down the steps to the cabin area below the poop deck. At the time she had idly wondered what he had been complaining about.

Captain Stark was not a man who

would accept anyone questioning his running of the ship. But that was the way of some of the cabin passengers Ellen had learned — spoilt, arrogant, used to having servants at their beck and call. Most of them tried to act as if the steerage passengers did not exist. She had not thought the doctor was one of them. But his manner as he had pushed past her, his handsome face flushed with temper, made her think otherwise.

And now, here he was, trying to tell her what to do. She pulled her arm away and spoke coldly. 'I heard the order and I am on my way down.'

'Well, hurry. They are waiting to close the hatches,' he snapped.

The storm had come up so suddenly that many of the steerage passengers had still been on deck, crowding the tiny area below the poop where they were allowed to get a little fresh air and exercise each day. Now it was almost deserted, washed by the sea as the ship dipped into another trough, and Ellen

4

realised she must hurry.

As she stumbled down into the dark well of the ship, she thought enviously of those better off than she, like the man who had just spoken to her. They had cabins shared with friends or family, not fifty or sixty strangers crammed together like roosting starlings. But she was lucky to be here at all, she supposed. Her brother-in-law had sent money towards her passage, though not enough to secure a cabin. But at least she had been able to buy a few comforts for the voyage.

She was the last one down and Mrs Jenkins, the matron, a thin pinch-lipped woman, who had been put in charge of the single women, gave her a push. 'Get in there with the other scum,' she snapped. A few days ago, Ellen would have snapped back, but she had learned the wisdom of keeping silent. As well as making sure the girls behaved themselves, Ma Jenkins was in charge of doling out the food and water. She had the power to make life even more miserable for those she took a dislike to.

Biting her lip, Ellen stumbled into the murky dimness, flinching as the huge wooden hatch cover closed over her head. The noise of the storm was muffled now and the creak and groan of ship's timbers was overlaid with the sobs and moans of the terrified emigrants. Through the noise she made out the voice of her friend, Millie. 'There you are, love. I were that worried about you — thought you'd been swept overboard.'

In the dim light of the swaying smoky lanterns Ellen studied the girl lying on the bunk in the corner they had made their own. Her face was pale, a bead of sweat along the upper lip, her hair lank and straggly over her shoulders. Beside her, another young woman held her hand, eyes round in her frightened face. Ellen, breathing shallowly through her mouth, attempted a smile. 'You'll not get rid of me that easy,' she said.

She crawled into the narrow space beside them. 'How are you feeling now?' she asked.

'I'll be better once I get off the ship,' Millie said.

'If we ever do,' the other girl said. 'I feel as if I've spent my whole life in this hole.'

'It's not worse than the hole you left behind, Joanie.'

'Aye, but that one at least kept still,' Joan replied.

Ellen smiled sympathetically. During their brief friendship she had learned much about the girls' former lives and she could understand their desperate need to seize the opportunity of bettering themselves on the other side of the world. The government assisted passage to Australia offered them their only hope of escape from poverty and degradation.

'Is there any water?' she asked.

Joan dipped a cupful out of the bucket in the corner. 'There's only a drop,' she said.

'We'd better not use too much then,' Ellen replied, pouring some back. She took a sip herself, then put her hand under Millie's head and put the cup to her lips. When she'd drunk her fill, Ellen moistened the corner of her shawl in the remaining dregs and gently wiped her friend's face.

'They'll be bringing more soon, and our food,' Joan said.

Ellen gagged at the thought of food but she shook her head. 'Last time they shut us in when there was a storm, it was days before we got anything.' She crawled in alongside her friends and pulled the thin blanket round her. 'Best try to sleep,' she said.

Trying to get comfortable on the hard plank bunk with its thin horsehair mattress, Ellen once more felt a pang of envy for the cabin passengers. They had their own kitchen and proper cooked food instead of the twice daily hunk of hard bread with a bowl of what passed for soup. Thanks to Patrick's money she had been able to buy extra supplies to supplement the meagre rations — hard biscuits, sugar, salt and a precious bottle of raspberry vinegar which she mixed with the water to take away the brackish taste.

When she had first come on board, greedy eyes had fastened on her box of provisions but thanks to Millie's intervention, no-one had dared come near. Growing up in the tough streets of London's East End, Millie had learned to fend for herself. In gratitude Ellen shared her things with the two girls who had befriended her.

They were just homeless girls who had fallen on hard times. Who knows what she would have been driven to herself if she had not had a sister and brother-in-law prepared to help her, she thought, as she finally drifted off to sleep.

She woke suddenly to cries of alarm. The lanterns were swinging wildly and the ship shuddered violently as it ploughed into another huge wave. Millie and Joan clung together, sobbing. Although terrified herself, Ellen tried to comfort them. Surely it could not go on much longer.

At last Joan and Millie fell into an uneasy sleep. But Ellen dared not close her eyes. Each time she did a wave of nausea swept over her and she was determined not to be sick. She fingered the letters in her pocket, creased and torn from repeated reading.

She knew them both by heart and as she repeated the words in her head she wondered yet again if she had done the right thing in agreeing to marry James. But she could not regret her decision to leave her old life behind for the new and strange land that lay ahead — that's if they ever got to Australia, she thought, as the ship dived into another trough with a scream of protests from ship's timbers and passengers alike.

But they'd survived the last storm and, as she strained her ears for sounds from on deck, it seemed to Ellen that this one was not as fierce as the previous one. At least the seas had not poured through the hatchway this time.

Surely they would come through it and she would see her beloved sister again. Once more she recited Mary's letter in her head.

My dear sister, although I have a good man to care for me and a better life than I could ever have hoped for in England, I miss you so much that it is as if I carried always a heavy stone which weighs me down with sorrow whenever I think back to the happy days of our childhood. Please make every endeavour to join me in this new land for although I may seem unhappy, I have no regrets concerning my decision to join my husband in this adventure. This is a good land with opportunities for all who have the will to work hard. My only sorrow was in leaving you behind.

Mary's husband, Patrick, had added a postscript to the letter, commending his brother, James, as a suitor and enclosing money to help with the journey to Sydney. What else could she do? With the death of her uncle, the sisters' only remaining relative, Ellen had found herself without a home or a job.

Caring for the cantankerous old man in his last illness had at least held the promise of a small legacy to keep her from destitution. But when the lawyers had finished there was nothing. With no references or experience Ellen's efforts to find work were doomed. She could have ended up on the streets like Millie and Joan. But the letter from Mary had arrived just in time, and with it the letter of proposal from James.

When her sister had married Patrick and declared their intention to emigrate, Ellen had been horrified. It was so different from the future they had envisioned for themselves as children. But who would have thought that they would have been left to fend for themselves at so young an age, dependent on the whim of their uncle?

The old man had declared she was marrying beneath her and would not get a penny of his money, but Mary loved Patrick and had defied him. From the letter she had received, Ellen thought her sister was happy, and she was glad, although she missed her badly.

The chance of joining her in her new life was tempting and, alone and destitute, Ellen told herself that marriage to a stranger would not be worse than the life she was living at present. Without taking time to think, she had gone to the shipping office to enquire about a passage. Arrangements made and the date for sailing fixed, she had written to both Mary and James of her eagerness to start her new life.

Joan turned over in the bunk and groaned and Ellen leaned over and took her hand. 'Try to sleep, Joanie. I think the storm's dying down. When you wake up it will be calm,' she said.

Millie sat up, rubbing her eyes. 'Oh, gawd, me stomach. If I'd know it would be like this I'd never 'ave come.'

'You don't mean that,' Ellen said. 'When they open the hatch and we get out on deck you'll feel better.'

'I'm not going up there again,' Millie said.

'Why ever not?' Ellen didn't understand. She couldn't wait to get out in the fresh air. Although at first the vast expanse of water and no sight of land had made her dizzy, she had come to love watching the play of light on the sea and the changing patterns of the clouds racing by above the billowing sails.

'We have to go through the married quarters to get up the stairs and I don't like the way those women look at me,' Millie said.

The few single women on the voyage were crammed into the bow of the ship well away from the men who were quartered at the other end, with couples and children between them. Ellen could understand Millie's feelings. Some of the married women had made nasty remarks about the type of people who were being allowed to colonise the new country. She had also born the brunt of their disdain because of her friendship with the two former street women, especially from Ma Jenkins.

'Take no notice of them, Millie. Act dignified and prove how wrong they are by your future behaviour.' It was good advice. Millie and Joan could easily have continued to ply their trade on board ship, as some of the other single girls did, despite Ma Jenkins' effort. But so far they had stayed true to their decision to give up the life and try to secure decent jobs when they arrived in Sydney. Ellen had to admire them and now she tried to help them by showing her friendship, even at the risk of ruining her own reputation.

'I hope it's not going to be like this when we get there,' Millie said.

'I don't think it will. My sister said in her letters that provided you are willing to work, your past is not important. People are judged on what they do, not like back home.'

'They say there's a shortage of

women too — maybe Joanie and me will get lucky and find ourselves a husband — like you.'

'I'm sure you will,' Ellen said, but at the moment she didn't feel so lucky. As the voyage progressed she felt more apprehensive. Soon she would come face to face with James, her sister's brother-in-law and there would be no going back.

'What's he like, this fiancé of yours? And what's he doing in Australia?' Millie asked.

'I've never met him.'

Joan groaned and sat up. 'What?' she said. 'Are you mad — a stranger?'

'Well, he's not exactly a stranger. My sister is married to his brother — and Patrick's a decent enough man. They've started a little store just outside Sydney — supplying the people who are settling in the wilderness. The outback they call it.'

'That sounds all right,' Millie said, with an envious smile. 'I could see meself running a store.'

'But you don't know him — he might be ugly or have smelly breath,' Joan said.

'He can't be any worse than some of the blokes we've dealt with,' Millie said.

Ellen felt herself blushing. 'Mary says he's very nice. And anything's better than being homeless or destitute.'

They all jumped as the hatch cover was thrown back, letting in a grey murky light.

The ship's mate slid down the companionway, using only his hands on the railings and stood looking round at the huddled pale-faced passengers.

'Any of you women done any nursing?' he bawled. Blank faces stared back at him. 'Come on, there must be one or two of you who knows how to look after a sick woman and child.' He stared round, hands on hips.

Millie pushed Ellen forward. 'Go on, you nursed your old uncle, didn't you?'

Ellen hesitated, not wanting to leave her new-found friends. But the mate saw her movement in the gloom.

'You there — yes, you. One of the cabin passengers needs help. Come on.'

Before she could protest he hustled her up the companionway on to the deck while the storm still lashed the rigging and white-capped waves sloshed over the side. The sailor grabbed her arm and pushed her through a door below the poop deck. It crashed shut behind them and he barred it with a baulk of timber.

It was quieter now and as they stumbled down a narrow passage towards the private cabin he said, 'The lady is Mrs Arnold. She is travelling to join her husband who is an important government official in Sydney. She has a fever, and her child has been sick, too.'

'Has the doctor seen them?' Ellen asked. She didn't like the sound of the word fever.

'Her brother is the ship's surgeon, Doctor Gray. It was he who asked for a nurse. As you can imagine, he is kept busy with many other patients under his care. He cannot be with her at all times.'

He paused outside a cabin door and knocked. Ellen took a deep breath, praying the fever was not something contagious. Besides, it seemed she had no choice.

2

The *Caroline* plunged into another wave and Ellen stumbled as she entered the cabin. Doctor Gray was bending over the lower bunk but he straightened and turned as the mate said, 'Here's the nurse, sir.'

Ellen recognised the man who had spoken to her on deck the previous day. He did not look so handsome now, his collar awry, sweat streaking his face and his eyes red-rimmed from lack of sleep. 'Thank the Lord,' he murmured, taking a step towards her.

'What do you wish me to do?' she asked.

'You have experience of nursing, Miss . . . ?'

'Ellen Campbell. I looked after my uncle before he died. But I would not call myself a nurse, sir,' she said.

'No matter. You are no stranger to a

sickroom and that is all that matters. My sister has a fever . . . No, no, it is nothing contagious,' he reassured her stretching out a placating hand. 'She has suffered from sea-sickness since the voyage began and now she is weak and feverish.'

Ellen looked down at the woman on the bunk. She lay with her knees drawn up to her chest, her thin hands clutching the blanket. Her eyes were closed and her hair lay in sweat-darkened strands across her forehead. She had delicate features and, when she suddenly opened her eyes Ellen saw in the light of the lantern that they were a vivid cornflower blue, just like her brother's.

'I have other patients to attend to, otherwise I would stay with her myself,' the doctor said. 'All you need to do is sit with her, bathe her forehead from time to time and see that she drinks as much as possible.' He indicated the bowl and pitcher on the shelf above the bed.

Ellen looked at the woman and felt a little burst of annoyance. She was only suffering from seasickness like so many on this voyage and she was better off than Millie and Joan. She had her own cabin, a plentiful supply of water and, now, someone to wait on her hand and foot.

She was about to say so and demand that she go back to her friends, when the woman reached out a thin hand and clutched at Ellen's arm. 'Thank God you are here,' she whispered. She looked over Ellen's shoulder to where the doctor stood by the cabin door. 'Richard, we shall be all right now.'

'We?' Ellen looked round and saw for the first time that there was another small bunk built across the narrowest part of the cabin. What she at first took for a pile of dirty laundry now stirred and a small fair head poked out. A pair of blue eyes gazed at her through a tangle of curls.

'Are you going to look after us?' the little girl asked. 'Mama is very sick.'

Ellen couldn't help smiling. 'Yes, I'll look after you,' she said.

The doctor nodded. 'Good. I'll be back later.' He closed the door behind him.

Ellen went over to the child, who was about four years old, and crouched beside the bunk. 'You're not sick too, are you?'

'My tummy hurts, but I feel better now I've had a sleep. I wish the boat would stop though.'

'The storm is nearly over. But we won't stop for a long time. It's a long way to Australia.' Ellen straightened the rumpled covers and plumped up the pillows. 'What's your name then?'

'I'm Amelia Arnold and I'm going to Australia to see my papa.'

'Well, Amelia, I'm going to look after you and your mama until you feel better.' She turned back to the bunk where the sick woman lay. 'Let's try to make you comfortable, Madam,' she said.

It did not take long for Ellen to

change the damp sheets and Mrs Arnold's nightgown, to bathe her face and brush the tangled hair. Now she looked much better and she struggled to sit up. 'Thank you,' she whispered. 'I am so grateful to you. You did not have to come.'

Ellen did not say that she felt she had had no choice in the matter. She held Mrs Arnold's head while she sipped some water, then eased the woman's head back on to the pillow. 'I'll just see to your daughter, then I must go back to my quarters. My friends will be wondering what has happened to me.'

'No, you must stay. I hate to be alone and Richard is so busy. Tell me a little about yourself. Why have you undertaken this voyage?'

Her voice was soft, pleading, not at all arrogant like her brother's, and Ellen found herself telling Mrs Arnold about her sister and brother-in-law's store in the small settlement outside Sydney and how much she was looking forward to joining them in their venture.

Afterwards, she wondered why she did not mention James, the man she was going to marry.

Although the storm had seemed to be dying down, by the next day the winds were as fierce as ever, and Mrs Arnold and her daughter succumbed to sea-sickness once more. Ellen was kept busy emptying the slop buckets and cleaning up the little girl, who clung to her and cried whenever she tried to leave her.

Despite the stench and her own queasiness, Ellen began to realise how lucky she was to be there. During the weeks she had spent below decks with Joan and Millie, she had become used to far worse sights and smells. At least here there was a privy of sorts, tucked away in what she had at first thought was a cupboard.

She was able to empty the buckets and basins regularly without having to go up on deck, or worse, leaving them until the storm blew itself out. And Doctor Gray made sure that a supply of clean water was brought to them daily.

Mrs Arnold was not a demanding patient but Ellen was worried about the little girl. As the days passed Amelia became more listless, refusing to eat. She lay on her bunk, her thumb in her mouth, clutching a rag doll. In between looking after her mother, Ellen sat beside her stroking her hair, telling her stories and singing the songs she remembered her own mother singing to her.

The days passed in a blur until Ellen could imagine no other life but this — the muted roar of the storm, the plunging of the ship, dozing whenever she could, and trying to comfort mother and child when she herself was feeling ill and terrified. And all the time she worried about Joan and Millie. How were they faring in the close confinement of the dark steerage quarters?

She had fallen into a light doze on the small bunk, her arm around Amelia, the little girl snuggled up against her in a deep sleep. The cabin door opened and she stirred, trying to sit up without disturbing the child. Something was different and it took a moment for her to realise what it was — the silence and the stillness. A smile crept across her face. The storm was over at last.

Doctor Gray stood in the doorway. He looked haggard and drawn, his shirt was wrinkled and sweat-stained and his tie was askew. He nodded towards his sister. 'How is she?'

'Well enough, but she is weak from having eaten nothing. Your niece too,' Ellen said.

'There is no sign of fever?'

'No, they are both sleeping normally now.'

A look of relief passed across his face but he stayed in the doorway. 'And you? Are you well?' he asked.

Something in his face stopped the sarcastic comment that rose to her lips. Instead she just nodded. 'I'll be all right, especially now that the storm is over.'

'I can't thank you enough for your care of my sister. I did not want her to make this voyage but she insisted it was her duty to join her husband.' His voice was weary, not the confident arrogant tone she had come to expect from him.

'I am sure they will both make a quick recovery now. They will be able to eat a little and regain their strength.' Ellen stood up. 'They will have no further need of my services so, if you permit me, sir, I will rejoin my friends.'

Richard Gray's lips tightened. 'I'm afraid that will not be possible. You must remain here.'

Ellen's quick temper rose. 'I am not your servant, sir. I stayed to help your sister because I do not like to see anyone suffering. And the child needed someone to care for her. But you cannot keep me here.'

'You cannot go down there . . . '

Before he could continue, Ellen tried to push past him. 'You have no authority over me,' she snapped.

He grabbed her wrist. 'Listen to me.

I have no authority — but Captain Stark does. He will not allow the hatches to be opened.'

'But the storm has passed. Those poor people down there need fresh air and exercise after being shut up for so long. Imagine how it must be for them.'

'I can not only imagine, I have seen for myself,' Richard said, his face grim. 'But when I informed the captain of the situation, his response was to keep the steerage passengers confined.'

'But why?'

'There is a fever running rife through the ship. Several have succumbed already. At first they thought it was the seasickness but I soon realised it could be something worse.'

Ellen's face paled and she pulled away from his restraining hand. Her first thought was for her friends. 'Millie, Joan?'

Richard's harsh expression softened. 'Your friends? The older one is all right, but I am afraid the little one — Joan is it? — she is very sick. But her friend is doing her best for her. She asks me to say will you forgive her? She has taken some things from your box of stores — to help her friend, she said.'

'I must go to them,' Ellen said.

'Have you not been listening? You must stay here. The captain has decreed that all passengers — steerage and cabin — should be confined to prevent the infection spreading. You have no choice but to stay here.'

'But you move freely about the ship. Can you not say that I am your assistant? As you know, I am now experienced in nursing.'

'That is true — you have done well here. But the captain will not allow me to take an assistant from among the women passengers. It is against the rules and he is a stickler for the rules.' Richard's lips set in a grim line. 'Besides, you may not be concerned about catching the fever yourself. But I cannot allow you near my sister and my niece once you have been in contact with others. I would not risk their lives

30

and they may have need of your services again before this voyage is over.'

'But you have been among the sick,' Ellen pointed out. 'Besides, I need a change of clothes.' She glanced down at the soiled hem of her skirt, realising it had been some days since she had even had the chance to undress for bed.

'Maybe my sister can lend you something,' Richard said.

'I may be poor but I do not need another woman's cast-offs.' Ellen's voice rose. 'I have a change of clothes in my box below decks. You must let me fetch them.'

'I have already said you must not go below,' Richard said, grabbing her arm again. 'Have you not noticed that I did not approach the child or Mrs Arnold?'

'But you have been in contact with me,' Ellen said, glancing down to where his hand lay on her sleeve.

He snatched it away quickly, his face colouring. 'Forgive me.' He sighed and his voice softened. 'I have already spoken to the captain about his treatment of the steerage passengers. He wishes me to concentrate my efforts on the cabin passengers and the crew. If he will not allow me to treat the immigrants, I cannot see him letting you go down there.' He turned away. 'Nevertheless, I shall speak to him again. I cannot leave those poor people to suffer.'

Ellen could see that she had no choice but to remain in the cabin with Mrs Arnold and Amelia and she gave up the argument, though with bad grace.

When Amelia woke she was brighter than she had been for days. She sat up in the bunk and smiled, holding her rag doll up to the sunlight streaming through the port hole. Ellen tried not to think of her friends shut up with no light but that from the smoky lamps, forced to breathe in the stink of illness. She knelt upon the bunk beside the little girl and inhaled the fresh air, enjoying the sun sparkling on the waves. All too soon they might have to close them up again.

The door opened and Richard stood in the doorway. His hair was still awry and his shirt, open at the neck, was wrinkled and stained. He looked as if he had not slept for days and Ellen felt a twinge of unwilling admiration for his obvious dedication to his work. Was he really as arrogant as she had thought?

Amelia looked round and her face creased in a beam of delight. 'Uncle Richard, have you come to play with me?' she asked.

'No, my sweet, I am too busy. I just wanted to see how you and your mama were faring.' The little girl made to scramble down from the bunk. 'No, sweetheart, you must stay there.'

'But I want to come on deck with you and watch the sailors pulling on their ropes and listen to them singing.'

'I'm sorry, Amelia. You must remain in the cabin for a little longer. Miss Campbell will play with you.' He glanced at Ellen. 'She seems to have made a quick recovery,' he said.

'I think everyone will feel better now that the motion of the ship has eased,' Ellen said. 'I am still a little worried about Mrs Arnold, though.'

Richard took a step forward but did not fully enter the cabin. 'Surely, she is just sleeping. That is all she needs now that the sickness has passed. She will soon recover her strength now.'

Ellen was not so sure but she did not want to worry him. He was probably right and rest was all she needed. She smiled. 'I will try to get her to eat when she wakes.'

'Good. I will ask the cook to send a little broth now that he is able to light the stoves once more.'

As he made to turn away Ellen forced herself to ask the question she had been dreading. 'What of the steerage passengers?'

'The captain has allowed the hatches to be opened to let in some fresh air — at my insistence I might add. But while there is still danger of contagion, no-one is allowed on deck.' He lowered his voice with a glance at Amelia. 'There have been several deaths unfortunately.'

'Who? Oh, please not Joan or Millie?'

'I guessed you would be worried about your friends and I asked the matron. They are both well, although weak.'

'I wish I could see for myself,' Ellen murmured.

'Be thankful you were not shut up down there with them,' he said. 'I have been able to see that they are provided with water but little more. From what I was able to see the situation is not a pleasant one.'

He stepped into the corridor, his hand still on the door. 'The good news is that the fever seems to be abating somewhat. The matron informs me there have been no new cases and those that were not too badly afflicted are already on the way to recovery.'

'Thank God,' Ellen said. Before he could walk away, she spoke again.

'Doctor Gray, what was the cause of the fever? If someone brought an infection on board before we left port, why did it not break out earlier?'

'I cannot say. I have given it much thought and intend to make a study of such matters in the future. I shall need to speak to other medical men and collect statistics and collate the various signs and symptoms of the disease.'

'So you will not be setting up in practice near your sister's new home?' Ellen asked, feeling a pang at the thought.

'I had intended to do so, but to make a proper study and try to solve the mystery of these outbreaks, I must return to London to consult with colleagues.' He gave a small laugh. 'But who knows what the future holds? First I must endeavour to see that as many passengers as possible arrive safely in their new home — if the captain will let me.'

'I am sure you will do your best, Doctor,' Ellen said.

'As you will for my sister and her child, I trust,' he said.

And then he was gone, leaving Ellen a little breathless. She wasn't quite sure what had happened during their exchange. But she was beginning to realise that Doctor Gray was not as arrogant or superior as she had first thought. His abrupt manner and barely suppressed anger were also far from being his true nature.

3

Later when Mrs Arnold and Amelia were both asleep, Ellen settled on to the top bunk beside the open port, enjoying the light breeze that played on her face. She too was exhausted after the storm-tossed days but now that she had the opportunity to rest she found she could not settle.

During the last few days she had become very fond of Amelia and of her mother too. Close confinement in the small cabin had led to an exchange of confidences that would have been unthinkable in other circumstances. Amelia, with no prejudices about class distinctions, had chatted freely about her life in England — the large house in Kensington, the country manor house where they had stayed with her grandfather before leaving for Australia.

Mrs Arnold was not as confiding as

her daughter and still seemed rather reserved, but she pressed Ellen to call her Jessie, and treated her more as a friend than a servant. Ellen knew it would not last once they were on dry land once more. Jessie would join her husband and begin a life of Government House receptions, tea with other ladies of rank — just like back in England. But she found herself responding to the other woman's gestures of friendship and had freely told her about her former life and her hopes for a new and better life in Australia.

She had nothing to hide after all and, were it not for the death of her parents and the change in her fortunes, she too might have married well and enjoyed the same status as the doctor's sister. But despite her willingness to share the details of her life, Ellen could not bring herself to confess that she was pledged to marry a man she had never met.

Lying on the bunk, her thoughts in turmoil, Ellen was forced to face the fact that she was no longer looking forward to meeting the man she was to marry.

She had liked the idea of two sisters married to two brothers, running a business together, bringing up their families in an exciting new land. It was true she had never met James but she had got to know and like Patrick shortly before he and Mary left for Australia. Surely James could not be too different from his brother? Now though, whenever she thought of James, it was Richard's face she saw in her mind's eye.

The sky outside the port was now a deep velvety black, studded with stars, an unfamiliar sky she now realised. She sighed, wondering if she would ever see the familiar constellations again. She pulled the shutter across, closing it firmly in case the seas got up again during the night. She lay down and, exhausted at last, fell into a deep sleep.

It was still dark when Amelia woke her, tugging at her hair, whispering.

'Mama is sick again.'

She lay for a few moments trying to get her bearings. Something was different, something about the ship. She sat up, rubbing her eyes. The cabin was hot, airless, and her body felt clammy. She swung her legs down from the bunk and gently guided Amelia back to her bed, tucking her in firmly. 'Don't worry, I'll see to her,' she said.

As she bent over the lower bunk she heard a faint whimper. Jessie seemed to be asleep but she was sobbing. Ellen got a damp cloth and bathed the other woman's face, stroking the hair back from her forehead and murmuring words of comfort.

Gradually the sobs eased and Jessie fell into an uneasy sleep, her head turning this way and that. Ellen heard the mumbled words, 'My baby, oh, my baby.'

She stayed beside the bunk, holding Jessie's hand until morning, when Amelia came and laid a hand on her shoulder.

'Mama is not going to die, is she?' the little girl asked.

Ellen turned and hugged her. 'Of course not, sweetheart. She's just tired and worn out with the voyage. She will be better once we reach Australia,' she said, trying as much to reassure herself as Amelia.

'Will we get there soon?'

'I don't know. We'll ask your uncle when he comes.'

'Perhaps we can ask him why the ship is not moving as well,' Amelia said.

It was true, Ellen realised. The regular rise and fall as the ship plunged through the waves was now replaced by a gentle scarcely-felt movement. There was a deathly silence too — no more slapping and snapping as the huge sails filled with wind, no creaking of ropes.

Had they reached land? The thought died at once. A busy port would be noisy, filled with bustle and clatter. Besides, Ellen knew that it would be many more days, maybe weeks before they reached landfall, especially as these days the ships took a different route, no longer sailing down the coast of Africa to stop at Cape Town.

From the heat and lassitude she was feeling she guessed they had reached the area called the doldrums where ships could be stuck for days.

'I think we are becalmed,' she said.

'What does that mean?'

'There is no wind to move the ship along,' Ellen explained.

She unfastened the port cover, hoping for a breath of fresh air. But all was still as she gazed out upon a flat sea and a sky burnt white by the fierce glare of the sun. The creak of a rope, a shouted order from the poop, and the ship seemed to lean over a little. But the movement did not last and all was still again.

Jessie woke and managed to get out of bed. She was still weak from her earlier sickness, but Ellen was pleased to see that she looked refreshed by her sleep and the dream which seemed to have caused her tears did not appear to have affected her.

Jessie had no more bad dreams but she grew quiet and introspective, spending long hours on her bunk, dozing or gazing out of the port hole at the unchanging vista of the ocean. 'It is this interminable heat,' she said when Ellen asked if she was feeling well.

But Ellen was sure there was something else troubling her. Surely it was not just the oppressive weather causing those dark shadows under her eyes and the sudden bouts of irritability. Luckily, Amelia was not a demanding child and did not pester for her mother's attention. The little girl seemed content with her own company, talking to her doll or looking at the picture books she had brought with her, and leaving her mother to rest.

But as the days passed and still the ship remained becalmed, the occupants of the small cabin grew fractious and snappy with each other. Earlier in the voyage one of the passengers, terrified of the huge waves, cried out he would not have come had he known of such peril.

Ellen had smiled when a crew member, an old salt, lined and weather-beaten from his years at sea, had laughed coarsely and warned, 'You'll have something to complain of when we reaches the doldrums, my lad. You'll be wishing for a gale force wind and a following sea then.'

Now she knew what he meant. The monotony of the long tedious hours was broken only by the arrival of their meals and the irregular visits of Richard Gray.

Ellen found herself looking forward to his visits although she knew she should suppress the feelings he aroused in her. He was pleasant — even friendly — but she knew he had no interest in her other than as the nurse who cared for his beloved sister and niece. Besides, he had told her he would be returning to England and she was betrothed to another man. There was no future in it. But through the long nights, sleepless in the heat, she could not help dreaming.

On the eighth windless day, Jessie had roused herself from her torpor to sit on the lower bunk and look at a picture book with Amelia, while Ellen sat with a torn petticoat in her hand, the needle still, unable to make the effort to continue with her mending. Even the fiercest storm would be preferable to this, she thought.

She looked up eagerly as the cabin door opened. A telltale blush stained her cheeks as Richard entered and she hastily dropped her eyes to her needlework.

To her surprise he did not linger in the doorway as usual but came right in, bending and lifting Amelia in his arms. 'And how is my sweetheart today?' he asked, swinging her up and kissing her cheek.

'I am well, Uncle. But I wish the ship would move again. I am growing weary of looking at all this sea.'

Richard gave a hearty laugh and set the little girl down. He sat down next to his sister and took her hand. 'And you, my dear. I hope you are feeling better now.'

'A little,' Jessie said, smiling. 'I too am weary though — of being confined in this dreadful cabin.'

'That is what I have come to tell you. The captain has agreed that you may go out on deck for a while.'

Ellen looked up eagerly. 'Do you mean the danger of infection has passed?'

'One can never be sure with these strange fevers. But there have been no new cases, although there is still much sickness, especially among the steerage passengers.'

'What of my friends?' Ellen asked.

'They are reasonably well — and they too, will be allowed on deck for a short while, so you may see for yourself.'

Ellen was overjoyed and would have rushed out immediately. But Richard put out a hand to stop her. 'The cabin passengers will go first, then Captain Stark has agreed that the mothers and children should come up from below. The single women will be allowed up next, then the men. He refuses to have all and sundry running about the ship and getting in the way of his men.'

'Can we go out now, Uncle?' Amelia asked.

'You may.' He turned to Ellen. 'May I suggest you keep an eye on her while my sister and I take a turn round the deck? Amelia will be keen to run about after being cooped up for so long and may prove too lively for Mrs Arnold.'

Ellen took the little girl's hand and followed them out into the fresh air, although it was really no fresher than inside the cabin.

It was hot and still, without the vestige of a breeze. Not a cloud marred the brassy sky and scarcely a ripple disturbed the vast expanse of ocean. But to Ellen it was a breath of heaven. She had always been a lover of the outdoors and had hated the move to the city to care for her uncle. Part of the attraction of Australia had been the opportunity to live in a land unmarred by the smoke and grime of the city.

As she walked round the deck, keeping a tight hold on Amelia's hand, the little girl skipped along, excited by the prospect of a change of scene. Around them, the crew members hurried about their business, swarming up into the rigging, pulling on ropes, furling and unfurling the different sails in an attempt to catch the slightest breath of wind. To no avail.

Ellen strolled along the deck, oblivious to the bustle around her, her eyes fixed on the back of the tall, fair-haired figure who filled her dreams. If it were not for the discomfort of the heat and humidity, she would not care if they continued to float in this silent world for eternity, she thought. The excitement and anticipation of an adventurous life on a new continent had diminished now that she had fallen in love.

All too soon they had to return to their cabin and Richard left to go about his duties. On long voyages like this there was always work for a doctor even when there was no epidemic to contend with. Several of the passengers had been ill when they arrived on board having been prescribed a sea voyage as a cure, although in many cases it seemed not to be working. And among the crew there were always broken bones and other injuries to keep him busy.

Amelia was lively and chatty and reluctant to return to the confinement of the cabin once more, but Ellen promised her another walk later in the day. She was more concerned about Jessie. Far from being revived by her brief excursion, she seemed exhausted and sank on to her bunk with a groan.

Ellen, feeling that she deserved a little time to herself, had hoped that Jessie would entertain Amelia while she sought out her friends. 'Is there anything I can get you?' she asked.

'Just leave me alone. I want to sleep,' Jessie moaned.

'But Mama, I wanted you to read to

me,' Amelia complained.

'I'm too tired.' Jessie turned to face the wall and covered her face with her hands.

'Maybe Mama will feel better when she has had a sleep,' Ellen said, trying to smile. She was worried about Jessie.

Richard had assured her that his sister was only suffering from the after effects of seasickness coupled with the discomfort of the long voyage. But Ellen was sure there was something more. She remembered the night she had been woken by Jessie's sobs but it was not her place to pry. She decided to speak to Richard when she had the chance and hoped that he would forgive her impertinence.

But snatching a moment alone with him was impossible. Perhaps it was just as well, Ellen thought, given the effect he had on her whenever he was near. Skin burning, pulse racing, she had never felt like this before.

She tried to distract herself by keeping Amelia amused but her heart leapt when the cabin door opened again and there he was. 'Your friends have come up on deck,' he said.

She jumped up eagerly but then looked at Jessie's sleeping form. 'I can't leave Amelia,' she said.

'Don't worry about her. There is a family across the way with two children about her age,' he said, bending and taking Amelia's hand. 'Would you like some other children to play with?'

Amelia went with him willingly and he turned to Ellen. 'Spend as much time with your friends as you wish. It will do Jessie good to sleep. Time is the best healer.'

There was no chance to ponder what he meant as she went out on to the small deck space in front of the cabins. The women from steerage milled around, some staring listlessly at the sea, others laughing and turning their faces up to the sun. They were a sorry looking crowd, their skin grey, hair lank and greasy.

Ellen spotted her friends leaning on

the rail and went towards them. Millie had her head thrown back, drinking in the air and light. But Joan clutched at the rail, hardly able to stand.

'Joanie, oh, you poor thing. Are you all right?'

'Better than I was,' Joan said with a valiant attempt at a smile. 'Thank gawd I had Millie 'ere to look after me.'

'It's good to see you both,' Ellen said. 'I missed you.'

Millie gave a harsh laugh. 'I bet you didn't give us a thought — stuck up there with the nobs in a cabin.'

Joan laid a gentle hand on her arm. 'She didn't have any choice, Mill.'

Millie shrugged. 'I guess not.'

'I wanted to visit you but I wasn't allowed. But I prayed for you every day,' Ellen said.

'Well, seems like your prayers were answered — we're still here, aren't we?' Millie put her hand on Ellen's arm. 'Don't mind me, love. I just feel angry at the way we were treated.'

'Yes, Rich . . . Doctor Gray told me

that they wouldn't let you up on deck. We were confined to the cabin too . . . '

'Oh, yes, your doctor friend.' There was a faint sneer in Millie's voice.

'He did his best,' Joan said sharply. She turned to Ellen. 'Did he tell you we raided your stores? I hope you don't mind but we were desperate.'

'Of course I don't mind, we're friends aren't we?'

'Do you mean that?' Millie asked.

'Yes. I could not have endured this voyage without both of you,' Ellen said.

Millie's manner softened. 'I thought you wouldn't want to know us since you've been mixing with the nobs,' she said.

'Hardly mixing. True, I shared their cabin — through necessity. But I am little more than a servant.'

When Ma Jenkins strode up to them, bawling that it was time for the women to go below, Millie and Ellen each took an arm and helped Joan towards the companionway. But when Ellen made to follow her friends down to the women's quarters, the matron barred her way.

'Where do you think you're going, miss?'

'Back to my quarters of course.'

'Oh no. Doctor Gray has given orders that you are to share his sister's cabin for the rest of the voyage.'

Ellen gasped. The arrogance of the man. All her earlier resentment resurfaced. 'How dare he? I agreed to nurse Mrs Arnold and her daughter while they were ill. But they have no further need of my services and I wish to return to my friends.'

'You'd best take it up with the captain then — he's the one that agreed to it.'

'I certainly will.' Ellen turned and marched to the companionway leading to the upper deck, where she could see the captain and the mate deep in conversation. But at the foot of the steps she changed her mind about confronting Captain Stark and decided to have it out with Richard instead.

As she went in search of him she was fuming. Millie and Joan had disappeared into the bowels of the ship and had not heard the exchange. Now Millie would think she was right and that Ellen had deserted them in favour of new friends.

4

Richard was not in his own quarters, nor was he in the small cabin that had been allocated as a sickbay and dispensary. Sighing, Ellen made her way to the Arnolds' cabin.

Jessie had woken and was helplessly trying to placate a sobbing Amelia. 'Hush, dear. There's no need to cry — Ellen is here now.' She looked up and gave a tired smile. 'She thought you had left us. But I was sure you would not be so foolish as to leave the comfort of a cabin and return to . . . ' She waved a hand, her nose wrinkling.

Ellen, already seething, could not stop her angry outburst. 'I agreed to stay because you needed my help — and because your brother gave me no choice. But the sickness has passed. You no longer need me and I would prefer to be with my friends, however low you consider them.' She whirled round, determined to appeal to the captain. They could not make her stay, she was not a servant employed by them.

Amelia began to cry again and Ellen hesitated, unwilling to upset the little girl. But, fired up by Millie's scornful remarks, she wrenched open the cabin door and came face to face with Richard. Ignoring his protests, she pushed past him and ran out on deck.

Several of the cabin passengers were strolling about and, from a partitioned off area in the stern, she could hear the raucous shouts of the male steerage passengers who were hauling up buckets of sea water and dousing each other.

Ellen moved as far away from them all as she could and found a secluded corner where she could watch the crew at work. Even in the shade it was still hot. Her hair hung limp across her damp brow and her clothes felt as if they were glued to her body. Thanks to Jessie's generosity in passing on several of her own dresses, she would be able to change into fresh clothes when she went below. But, unlike the men, she could not indulge in a dousing with sea water.

She blamed the heat for her earlier outburst and wished she had not been so hasty. Jessie was right to think that the cabin was better than being quartered below deck — surely that was what she had meant. She had not been referring to Ellen's friends. Besides, hadn't she thought like that herself once upon a time — before the change in her circumstances that had left her penniless and alone?

She turned at a footstep on the deck and saw Richard approaching. As she went to move away, he took her arm. 'I'm afraid Jessie has upset you,' he said. 'You must forgive her. She did not mean to belittle your friends, but she has been used to being waited on by servants. Her upbringing has meant that she's never had to think about those less fortunate than herself.'

'In that she is no different from myself,' Ellen retorted, pulling away from him. 'But I have learned differently . . . ' She choked back a sob.

'She is truly sorry,' Richard said gently.

But Ellen was still feeling resentful. 'It wasn't only your sister who upset me.'

'Who else then?'

She glared at him and turned away.

He put a hand on her shoulder and turned her to face him. 'Miss Campbell — Ellen — surely I haven't done anything . . . '

'You stopped me going back to my friends. You had no right. I am not your servant, nor your sister's.'

'I can assure you I do not think of you as a servant. I merely thought you would be pleased to spend the remainder of the voyage in more comfortable surroundings. I wanted to show my gratitude for your care of my family.'

'I would like to have been consulted, that's all,' Ellen said more quietly.

'I see that now. But it was your welfare I was thinking of.'

Ellen bit her lip. She could not stay angry for long — especially when he was looking at her like that. Her stomach churned and when he said softly, 'Am I forgiven?' she could only nod, feeling the telltale blush sweeping over her whole body.

He bent his head towards her and she lifted her face to his. But as his lips brushed hers a footstep behind them made him jerk away. She turned towards the railing, gripping it with both hands, staring out at the burnished sea, trying to still the wild beating of her heart.

When she turned back, Richard was gone.

A sailor leapt on to the rail alongside her and began to swarm up the ropes to the yardarm high above. Another followed, and another. She gazed upwards, watching them diminish into black dots against the cloudless sky. And then she saw it, the movement of a sail, felt the tremor of the deck beneath her feet. Then ship was moving, there was a breeze, faint at first but growing stronger. Suddenly there was frantic activity, shouts and running feet.

A cheer went up from the men. They were out of the doldrums at last. The voyage was more than half done and in a few weeks they would reach Australia. But her heart was heavy as the thought that once they made landfall, she would never see Richard Gray again.

When Ellen returned to the cabin, Jessie added her apologies to Richard's and begged her to stay with them for the remainder of the voyage. But it was Amelia's pleas that swayed her and, against her better judgement, she agreed. She knew it would be hard to avoid Richard altogether, but she made up her mind never to be alone with him and to keep their encounters to a strictly professional basis.

The next few days passed pleasantly. With the freshening winds, the sails filled and the ship scudded along, skimming the waves like the huge strange birds which had appeared. There were also flying fish, whales and dolphins to entrance Amelia as they leaned on the rail. The doldrums were far behind them now and there was an air of lightheartedness among passengers and crew.

Ellen breathed in the fresh air and resolved to enjoy it while it lasted. She refused to dwell on what would happen when the ship reached Sydney and she would have to say goodbye to Richard forever.

Jessie was feeling so much better now that the oppressive heat had lessened and she was sometimes able to look after Amelia herself, leaving Ellen free to spend time with her friends. As soon as Millie and Joan came up on deck, she would join them and spend a pleasant hour, laughing and joking and speculating on the new country they were fast approaching.

Sometimes, Millie's coarseness shocked her, but she told herself it did not matter.

Her sister, Mary, had often said in her letters that class differences no longer mattered in Australia. It was willingness to work and contribute to the success of the colony that counted. And both Millie and Joan had declared their intention of doing just that.

She was standing with her back against the rail laughing at one of Millie's jokes, which Joan had just explained to her, when she caught sight of Richard. He was bending to examine a seaman who appeared to have been injured. His back was to her and she stared at him, foolishly willing him to turn round. But he was busy and did not seem to notice her.

But Millie laughed. 'Still mooning after the doctor, I see,' she said.

Ellen started to protest but Joan intervened. 'Leave her be, Millie. You shouldn't tease.' She turned and nudged Ellen. 'You can look now, he's gone.'

Millie was contrite. 'Sorry. But you're wasting your time, love. 'He's not for the likes of you.'

'I know that,' Ellen snapped. 'Besides, it's not what you think . . . '

'I've got eyes in me head, love. And I can see how you feel. Better not let him see it too, or he'll be taking advantage of you. That sort always do.'

'You're wrong, Millie. Anyway, haven't you forgotten? I'm getting married when we land.'

Millie's retort was lost in the shouts of the crew as they were given the order to shorten sail. The wind had increased and dark clouds were massing on the horizon. The brief spell of good weather was about to end. The steerage passengers were once more urged below to allow the sailors room for their manoeuvrings and Ellen reluctantly left her friends.

As she made for the passageway leading to Jessie's cabin, Ellen had to pass several of the ladies who had gathered to drink tea in the communal area which they had made their own. The conversation died away and one or two of them stared at Ellen. She knew they disapproved of her consorting with the lower classes as they put it.

'If any of them come into the store when I've settled in Sydney, I shall refuse to serve them,' she told herself. The thought gave her great satisfaction and she held her head high as she swept past, pretending she did not care.

The cabin door was ajar and Ellen hesitated when she heard Richard's voice. She was about to turn away when she heard Jessie's raised voice and, despite herself, she stayed to listen.

'You've seen for yourself, Richard. She spends all her time with those — women.' She almost spat the word. 'I've tried to be kind to her, and I don't deny that she has been a great help these past weeks. I did think that she was not like those others, despite throwing in her lot with them. But she is not our sort, you must see that.'

Ellen could not hear Richard's quiet reply, although she strained towards the door.

Then Jessie spoke again. 'It's your

happiness I am thinking of. You are a brilliant surgeon, you have a great future before you. I had hoped you would make a good marriage . . . '

'You cannot plan my life for me, Jessie. I have made my own plans.' His words came clearly now and Ellen realised he had moved towards the door. As she went to move away, she heard Jessie's protest.

'No, please tell me you have not made a declaration to her already.'

'Of course not. It would not be right.' His next words were a low murmur, but then Ellen heard him say loudly. 'It does not matter what you say or think, I am returning to England on the next ship.'

Ellen felt faint and she leaned against the bulkhead, trying to stem the tears that welled up. Hastily pulling herself together she continued down the passage, past the cabin. She could not face him now. He was going back to England and once the voyage was over, she would never see him again.

She heard the door close and Richard's footsteps receding. After a few moments she composed herself enough to enter the cabin and to enquire if Jessie needed anything.'

'No, thank you,' Jessie said abruptly.

Ellen nodded and made to leave, but Jessie held out a hand. 'Don't go, Ellen. I would like to talk to you.'

'Where is Amelia?'

'She is playing with the Simpson children in their cabin. We will not be disturbed.'

Reluctantly, Ellen sat down, picking up some mending she had left on the small bunk. She bent her head over the needlework, biting her lip. She knew what Jessie was going to say and she did not want to hear it.

'First, I must tell you how grateful I am for your care of me during my sickness, and for looking after Amelia. She has become very fond of you.'

'And I of her,' Ellen said.

'But you must see that, if you are to continue looking after her, I cannot allow you to be seen consorting with those . . . ' She struggled to find the word and Ellen interrupted hotly.

'Do you mean my friends? How dare you judge them — and me? When I came on board I knew no-one, I was alone and afraid. They helped me. Joan and Millie are my true friends.'

'You were forced into the company by circumstances — I understand that and I admire your loyalty. But you must see that they are not your kind of people.' When Ellen opened her mouth to speak, Jessie held up a hand. 'I know they say that it is different in Australia, that there is no difference in people's circumstances, it is a more free society than in England. But I cannot believe that the likes of those women will ever be invited to take tea at Government House.'

'And by association, you think that would apply to me also?' Ellen stood up, laying the mending down carefully. Her face was flushed and she dug her nails into the palms of her hands to prevent them from shaking. Her voice was icy calm as she faced the woman she had begun to think of as a friend. 'What makes you think I would ever want to be invited to such a gathering?'

Jessie met her gaze, 'If you were to marry my brother . . . '

A harsh laugh escaped her. 'From what I overheard, I think that is most unlikely, don't you?' she said.

And with that, she left the cabin and hurried out on deck. She paused by the rail, taking in deep breaths of the spume-laden air. The seas had got up even more in the past hour and it was noticeably colder. She shivered and pulled her shawl more closely about her, then made her way below.

Pulling aside the heavy curtain that shut off the women's quarters, she pushed between the bunks, ignoring the protests of Mrs Jenkins, the matron.

Joan looked up from brushing her hair and nudged Millie's arm. 'Look who's here,' she said.

'So — fallen out with yer new pals, 'ave her? I knew it wouldn't last.'

In answer, Ellen threw herself on to the lower bunk and burst into tears.

5

Ellen took a gulping breath as the sobs gradually subsided. She sat up, pushing her hair off her face.

Joan was beside her, a comforting arm round her shoulders. 'What's up, love?'

'It's that doctor, in't it? I told yer to watch out fer 'im,' Millie said. 'What's he done to yer, girl? I'll give him a piece of my mind if he's hurt yer.'

'It's not Richard. He's done nothing. I'm just being silly.' How could she tell them what Jessie had said without hurting their feelings? She managed a smile. 'I'm just so pleased to be back here with you — if you'll put up with me. I don't want to have anything more to do with that lot up there.'

'You sure?' Joan asked. 'It's not very nice down here, especially as you've got used to living with the nobs.'

'What happened then? Why did you change your mind and come back with us?' Millie asked.

'They don't need me any more now the sickness has passed. Besides, I didn't like being treated like a servant.' It wasn't quite true but they seemed to accept it.

They were interrupted by the appearance of Ma Jenkins. 'So, they threw you back in the cess-pit, I see,' she sneered. She stood with her hands on her hips, braced against the motion of the ship, waiting for a reply.

Ellen had always been aware of the woman's contempt for the single women, judging them all the same, despite their varied circumstances. But she stilled the angry retort that rose to her lips. There was no sense in annoying her when she had such power over them and could make their lives even more uncomfortable if she chose.

Keeping her dignity with difficulty she said, 'The Arnolds have no further need of my services now that they are full recovered and there is no further danger of infection.'

'Well, I don't want any more toing and froing — it unsettles the cabin passengers. They like people to know their place — and yours is here from now till we reach Sydney. And I shall tell Doctor Gray the same. I am sure Captain Stark will agree with me.'

Before any of them could reply, she was gone.

'Bossy old cow. What gives her the right . . . ?'

'Hush, Millie,' Ellen said, laying a hand on her arm. 'She's in charge of the stores and the water. No sense in upsetting her.'

'She's right,' Joan said. 'Come on, let's sort out these bunks and make room for Ellen.'

By the time they had sorted out their things and Ellen had checked the remaining stores in her chest, it was time to queue up on deck to collect their evening meal of stew and hard bread. As they waited their turn, Ellen looked up at the sails, bellying in the wind. The movement of the ship was even more pronounced and she dreaded the approach of another storm.

When they had finished eating, Ellen delved into her trunk and got out the bundle of letters. By the light of the smoky lantern she re-read James's proposal and her sister's heartfelt endorsement of his suitability as a husband. Mary was right, she told herself. She would have a good life in the new country and, once they arrived, she would put this awful voyage behind her.

As she folded the letters and put them away, Millie said, 'Having second thoughts, love?'

'Not at all. I was just reminding myself how lucky I am to have this chance of a new life.' She lay down in her bunk and pulled the covers over her.

As she drifted off to sleep, she heard Millie whisper. 'I'm sorry for being so horrible to you.'

The days settled into a pattern once

more and Ellen, by keeping busy, managed to banish Richard from her thoughts — at least during the day. It was different at night, especially when the weather worsened and the plunging of the ship as she ploughed through the heavy seas kept everyone awake. As the waves grew rougher, even those who had grown used to the ship's motion over the past few weeks suffered a recurrence of the seasickness.

Joan was badly affected and Ellen and Millie had their hands full cleaning up after her and trying to reassure her that she was not dying. Ellen couldn't help wondering how Jessie and Amelia were faring. Despite everything, she had become fond of them, especially the little girl. She half-hoped that she would be summoned to their cabin again. But after the way she had spoken to Richard's sister, she knew it was most unlikely.

Ellen woke one morning shivering and hoped she was not getting a fever. But as she swung her legs over the side of the bunk her bare feet recoiled. It was freezing. She thrust her feet into her shoes and pulled her shawl around her shoulders, careful not to disturb her friends. All was quiet save for the grunts and snores of the sleeping passengers.

Then she heard other noises — banging and a crackling sound, different from the usual groaning and creaking of the ship in full sail. There were shouts from above, running feet on the deck and a hammering and crashing.

'What now?' she muttered, cautiously mounting the steps and poking her head over the edge of the hatch. She could hardly believe the sight that met her eyes. Several inches of snow lay on the deck and the sails and rigging were stiff with ice. The ship was moving sluggishly and the men ran frantically here and there, using their axes to break the icicles which weighed down the rigging.

Ellen glanced up and gasped. Towering over the ship was a mountain of ice, higher than the highest mast, not pure white as she had imagined an iceberg, but shot through with streaks of turquoise and vivid blues and greens. It was so close that she felt she could almost reach out and touch it. Surely the ship would plough straight into it? But at the last moment, the vessel veered away and began to sail alongside.

She held her breath, willing them to pass in safety. Even when they had passed, she could not take her eyes off it. She had heard stories of ships ripped apart by icebergs but, despite her terror, she could see a stark beauty in the awesome sight.

Ellen shivered again and scrambled down the ladder into the relative warmth below. She hurried back to her bunk and pulled the blanket over her. Joan stirred and said, 'Morning already. Is it breakfast time?'

'Not yet. Stay in the warm. It's freezing on deck.'

'It's freezing down here,' Millie complained, stretching and sitting up. 'I ain't slept a wink all night.'

'I've been up on deck. It's been snowing and there's ice everywhere. I think they'll make us stay down here today.'

'Not too much to get up for,' Millie complained. 'They didn't tell us it would get this cold on the voyage.'

'I thought Australia was a hot place. Surely it should get warmer as we get nearer,' Joan said.

'It's to do with the winds,' Ellen said. 'We have to go further south than Australia and then north again.' She shook her head. 'It's hard to explain.' She felt a pang, remembering one of Richard's visits to the Arnold cabin. He had sat with Amelia on his knee, showing her on the atlas where they were going and the route the ship was taking. He had explained it all patiently and Ellen had listened with a smile on her face.

'Never mind all that,' Joan said, interrupting her thoughts. 'When are we going to get breakfast?'

As she spoke, the curtain was pulled back roughly and Ma Jenkins shouted. 'Come on you lazy lot, get up on deck. Your gruel's here. And be quick about it. The captain don't want you lot sliding around all over the place when he's got his ship to see to. You get your breakfast and get back down here.'

Ellen and her friends joined the shivering grumbling queue, grateful that at least the thin gruel was still fairly hot when they got theirs. Those further back in line would not be so lucky for the steaming cauldron was placed on the icy deck at the head of the companionway and was already beginning to cool.

Back in their little nest of blankets the girls ate their breakfast, then snuggled down hoping to find a degree of warmth in their closeness.

For the first time Ellen regretted her precipitous flight from the cosy Arnold cabin — not because of the comfortable berth she had left behind, but because she had not brought with her the things that Jessie had given her. At the time she had told herself she did want the other woman's castoffs. Now she thought longingly of the warm gowns, the fur-edged pelisse and the woollen stockings that would have helped to alleviate her present misery.

The cold got worse and Ellen stayed in her bunk trying to keep warm, listening to Joan and Millie as they sat round the central table playing a card game with some of the other young women. They were hunched over, blankets draped round their shoulders, indulging in their usual moans about the weather, the food, the matron, the other passengers.

Their voices faded away as Ellen started to doze. She was on the edge of sleep when she heard Richard's voice. She told herself she must be dreaming but still she sat up.

Ma Jenkins's voice rose. 'I didn't send for you, Doctor. There's no-one sick here,' she said.

'Let me pass, woman. I tell you I

have a patient to see to.'

Ellen's heart leapt as a figure pushed its way past the matron and, in the dim light of the smoky lamp, she saw that she had not been dreaming — it was Richard. Just a brief glimpse of him was enough to tell her that she had not put him out of her mind — and heart — as she had managed to persuade herself over the past few days. She wondered who was ill enough to need a doctor until she realised he had stopped at the foot of her bunk.

He bent towards her, concern in his eyes. 'Are you sick?' he asked.

'I'm just cold — as we all are,' she said.

'Oh, Ellen, you shouldn't be here,' he said softly.

The memory of him discussing her with his sister resurfaced and she could not respond to the kindness in his voice. Before she could stop to think, the angry words tumbled out. 'And why not? As Mrs Arnold so rightly said, I belong here — with my own sort.'

He recoiled a little at her harsh tone and his own voice hardened. 'I thought you would have need of your things.' He slammed the carpet bag he had been carrying on to the end of the bunk and strode away.

Ellen gazed after him, tears welling up. Why had she let her pride get the better of her? But then she brushed the tears away. Hadn't she resolved to forget him, to make the best of the opportunity she had been given to start life afresh in Australia?

Millie got up from the table and sauntered over. 'What did his nibs want then?'

'He brought some things I'd left in the cabin.'

Millie picked up the bag, fingering the tortoiseshell handles. 'Nice,' she murmured. 'I don't remember you having this before.'

'Mrs Arnold gave it to me.'

Joan joined them. 'Open it up then.'

'It's only my old cloak and gown that I left behind,' Ellen said. She had a feeling that the bag also contained the clothes that Jessie had given her, but although she had been grateful at this time, she now felt she could not accept anything from her. 'You open it,' she said to Joan, turning away.

Joan undid the clasp, gasping as she drew out the fur-edged pelisse that had belonged to Jessie Arnold. 'This isn't yours,' she said.

The old sneer was back in Millie's voice as she said, 'I didn't think you were the sort of girl to accept gifts from gentlemen.'

'I'm not. How could you think . . . ?'

'Well, he brought the bag, didn't he?'

'Jessie — Mrs Arnold — gave it to me.' Before Millie could say anything, she went on, 'You have it — it'll help keep you warm.' She delved into the bag and pulled out a warm woollen skirt. 'And you can have this, Joan.'

The two girls protested but Ellen persuaded them to accept the gifts. But when she tried to force the other items from the bag on them they refused.

'Don't be so stubborn,' Millie said. 'You need something warm to wear as well. Besides, you worked for them for weeks. You deserve something in return.'

Joan reached into the bottom of the bag. 'What's this?' she held up a folded sheet of paper. 'It's got your name on it, Ellen.'

'Ooh, a love letter,' Millie said, snatching it from her.

'Don't be silly,' Ellen said but her heart was beating faster. However, when Millie passed it to her she would not take it. 'You read it,' she said.

Millie unfolded it and ran her finger along the lines, her lips moving. 'I can't make it out,' she said, 'too dim in here.'

Ellen realised that Millie probably could not read very well and she took the paper from her As her eyes dropped to the signature at the bottom her heart fell. 'It's from Mrs Arnold,' she said.

'*My dear Miss Campbell*,' the note began. Ellen read it quickly, a stiff formal note asking her to accept the clothes in appreciation of the help she had given and wishing her well in the future. She seemed to have unbent towards the end for the last line read, *Amelia misses you*.

The bitter cold continued and the girls spent most of their time below deck now, huddled in their bunk and trying to keep warm. Now Ellen was grateful for the extra clothing that Jessie had given her and she noticed that there were no longer any sarcastic comments from Millie as the three of them struggled under the warm coat, wearing the extra petticoats and stockings that had also been in the bag.

The ship ploughed on through the ice pack in eerie silence, broken only by the shouts of the crew and the crackling of the ice. On their rare forays topside they gazed in awe at the majestic mountains of ice, sometimes sparkling in the sunshine, sometimes shrouded in mist.

Once, as they sat at the table eating their midday stew, there was an ominous scraping sound and the ship gave a great lurch. They held their breath, clutching their soup bowls and gazing upwards in fear. Several of the young women began to cry and one or two even rushed towards the companionway, certain that the order would be given to take to the boats. But there were only the usual shouted commands from the officers and the scurrying of feet on deck. Gradually, they relaxed and went back to their food.

Then came the morning when Ellen woke and noticed a difference in the ship's movement. She was sure the temperature seemed to have risen a little as well. It was still cold, though, she thought, as she got out of the bunk and put on her shoes. She did not need to dress for she was already wearing all the clothes she possessed. No-one else was awake and she cautiously went through the married quarters, anxious to avoid Ma Jenkins and her hectoring voice.

The hatch was already open and she could hear voices from above. As she climbed the ladder a shaft of sunlight almost blinded her and she thought she could feel a little warmth. As she emerged on deck she realised this was an illusion. The wind cut like a knife, even through the many layers of clothing she wore.

But they were out of the ice. The deck was awash with the slushy residue of melting snow and from the rigging icy droplets fell like rain, sparkling like so many jewels in the sun. Ellen tilted her face upwards and breathed in the fresh air, like nectar after so long breathing the foul air below.

The wind grew stronger and Ellen saw that the waves, capped with white foam, were huge. The crew began to haul on the ropes at a shouted order from the captain on the quarterdeck above Ellen's head.

As they pulled, they sang one of the shanties that had become familiar over the months they had been at sea. She found a sheltered corner, careful to keep out of the way of the seamen.

The door leading to the first class cabins was open but there was no-one about this early. Ellen's relief that she was unlikely to encounter Richard was mixed with disappointment. But what could she say to him if they did meet?

The sun suddenly disappeared behind a great cloud and the brief spell of fine weather ended abruptly. As Ellen turned to go below, a cry reached her ears. 'Ellen, wait for me.'

It was Amelia. The little girl, clutching her doll, emerged from the shadows below the poop deck. As she ran towards Ellen across the slippery deck, the sails filled and the ship lurched forward. Ellen held out a hand, helplessly watching as the child skidded and fell.

She ran towards her but the ship plunged into another wave and she stumbled. When she had righted herself she looked again and Amelia had disappeared. With a gasp of horror she ran towards the spot where she had last seen her.

The ship was plunging more violently now and water was slopping over the sides. Ellen caught a glimpse of a small white hand clutching at a stanchion and she threw herself towards it, grabbing at the child as another wave swept over them. She managed to clasp a trailing rope and held on until the ship righted itself again.

Gasping, she pushed herself upright, holding on to Amelia with all her strength. She knew she must reach the shelter of the overhanging poop before the next wave came or she would be swept overboard with the child.

Despite the weight of her wet clothing holding her back, she managed to struggle towards the doorway. As she reached its shelter, a figure reached out and grabbed at her. 'What on earth are you doing out here?' a voice shouted in her ear.

Richard pushed her into the cabin and took the child from her. The whiteness of Amelia's face was broken only by the livid bruise across her forehead. Her eyes were closed and, as Richard laid her gently on the bunk, Jessie cried out in alarm, 'Oh, my poor baby.' She turned accusingly to Ellen. 'What have you done to her?'

Ellen, shivering in her wet clothes, only stared dumbly, praying that Amelia was not dead.

Before she could speak, Richard said, 'She has saved your daughter's life. What were you doing letting her go out on deck alone?'

'I was asleep,' Jessie mumbled.

They all turned as the little girl stirred on her bunk. 'I was looking for Ellen. Mama would not wake up and I was lonely. I wanted her to play with me.' Her eyelids fluttered and she murmured, 'I'm tired now.'

'Well, before you go to sleep we must get your wet clothes off and warm you up.' Richard finished his examination and turned to Jessie. 'No harm done, it's just a bruise.'

'Thank God,' Jessie said, kneeling beside the bunk. She gently took off the child's wet clothes and wrapped her in a blanket. Holding her close, she turned to Ellen. 'I don't know what to say. If you had not been there . . . '

'It was purely by chance. If it had been a few minutes later . . . ' Reaction to what had happened caught up with her and she faltered. Her legs felt weak and she grabbed the door jamb.

Richard took her arm. 'Sit down — and get those wet things off. You're shivering.' He turned to Jessie and spoke sharply. 'Find something for her to wear while I go to the galley and get some hot broth.'

'I'll be all right,' Ellen said. She turned to go back to her own quarters but her legs would not move. When Richard returned carrying a pan of steaming broth, she was still holding on to the door, her teeth now chattering loudly.

'Jessie, can't you see that Ellen needs help. Leave Amelia to sleep and find some dry clothes for her,' Richard said. He prised Ellen's hand away from the door and forced her to sit on the lower bunk. 'You must take those things off or you will be ill,' he said. 'I'll come back in a minute.'

By the time he came back, Ellen had managed to strip off and wrap herself in a blanket. Her clothes were in a heap on the floor. She was still shivering but gradually life was returning to her frozen hands and feet.

Jessie had not moved. She was still holding Amelia, rocking her in her arms like a baby and Richard did not comment. He poured some broth into a bowl and sat beside Ellen, holding up the spoon. She opened her mouth obediently, but after a few mouthfuls she pushed him away and tried to get off the bunk.

'No, you must stay here until you are fully recovered. Jessie will look after you.' He glanced across at his sister and raised his voice. 'Amelia is quite safe now. She needs to sleep and recover from her ordeal. Come here, Jessie, and persuade Ellen to take some more broth. I must go and see if I have any more patients this morning.'

He turned at the door and spoke to Ellen. 'I will tell your friends what has happened so that they will not worry.'

She managed to smile but words would not come. Her eyes closed and she slipped into a deep sleep.

When she woke, the cabin was dark. As she sat up, she was aware of a figure sitting next to the bunk. She heard movement, a muffled exclamation and the sound of the lamp being lit. Richard leaned towards her and put a cool hand on her forehead.

'Good,' he murmured. 'No fever.'

'I feel quite well now. I'll return to my quarters,' she said.

'I wish you would stay,' he said.

Ellen's heart leapt but at his next words she realised he had not meant it quite the way she had hoped.

'I think Jessie needs you. She is not well and I worry about her fitness to care for Amelia. Today's incident was no accident,' he spoke quietly, with frequent glances across the cabin.

Ellen looked and realised that Jessie was not in her own bunk. She was still sprawled, half lying, half kneeling, beside her daughter, her arms round the little girl. It looked as if she had not stirred for hours.

Despite her resolve to have nothing more to do with this family, Ellen's tender heart was moved. Hadn't she wondered about Jessie's frequent bouts of melancholy, her headaches and lassitude? She had often felt it was more than the rigours of the voyage which ailed her.

'What do you mean? Amelia woke early and wandered out of the cabin. It is nobody's fault.' Ellen shuddered at the thought of what might have happened. 'I am just thankful I was there.'

Richard took her hand. 'I can't thank you enough.' He sighed and let go. 'Poor Jessie has had a hard time since her husband left to take up his appointment in Sydney.'

'Why did she not travel with him?'

'She was with child. My brother-in-law could not delay his departure and it was agreed that she should join him after the baby was born.'

'She lost the baby?' Now Ellen knew the meaning of those nights when Jessie had awoken her with her desperate sobbing.

'My poor sister was distraught. She was ill for months.' He sighed again. 'She did not want to make the journey, especially when her maid left us. But I persuaded her that she was well enough. Foolishly, I thought that having to care for Amelia by herself would take her mind off her grief.'

'I knew there was something wrong. But she seemed much better . . . '

'I thought she was. But this latest episode . . . ' He ran his hands through his hair. 'She had taken laudanum. That is why she did not wake when Amelia ran out the cabin.'

Ellen nodded as Richard explained how he prescribed the drug to help his sister sleep and to cope with her grief. But he had feared she was becoming dependent on it and had stopped giving it to her. But somehow she had managed to get hold of a supply.

'I can't watch her all the time, Ellen. I have my duties to attend to. I know it is a lot to ask after the way she treated you. But I need someone I can trust.' He glanced across at the smaller bunk. 'And so does Amelia.' He took her hand again. 'Please stay.'

Against all her instincts, Ellen nodded. 'I'll stay — for Amelia,' she said.

6

There were many times in the next few days when Ellen wished she had not given in to Richard's plea. As the *Caroline* plunged through the roaring forties, once more beset by terrible storms, it was impossible to leave the safety of the cabin. Jessie, once the effects of the laudanum had worn off, became irritable, making unpleasant comments about Ellen's choice of friends and snapping at Amelia.

Even the noisome conditions below deck would be preferable to this abuse, Ellen thought, when once again Jessie was being particularly objectionable. At least she would be with her true friends. She was worried about them too.

'They are quite well — except for seasickness. I will pass on your good wishes,' Richard promised when, at the height of the storm, she anxiously enquired how Millie and Joan were faring.

Ellen smiled and thanked him. Their exchanges had been stiff and formal since he had confided his sister's problems to her. He was probably embarrassed to have revealed so much and she, for her part, had decided that she would conduct herself as if she were indeed merely a nursemaid and companion to the Arnolds. After all, she told herself frequently, she was engaged to be married and her thoughts should be only of James and her forthcoming marriage.

Despite her resolve though, Ellen lived for these brief exchanges with Richard. She knew she should not have agreed to stay and frequently told herself it was only for Amelia's sake that she did not insist on rejoining her friends. But she could not deny how her heart leapt with a mixture of pleasure and pain whenever she looked up and saw his tall figure framed in the doorway.

The voyage had lasted for almost four months but to Ellen it seemed as if they had been at sea for far longer. The days dragged by in a fog of boredom, alternated with misery and discomfort. How much longer would it be?

Jessie had succumbed to another bout of depression and was lying on her bunk. Ellen had given up trying to engage her interest in anything and was trying to keep Amelia amused, when they heard shouts from aloft. 'Land ho, land to port.'

She leapt up in excitement but a roll of the ship sent her sprawling back on her bunk. She struggled upright and caught hold of Amelia's arm as the child started to run towards the door.

'Wait, sweetheart,' she said.

'But the man said 'land'. We must be there at last.'

'It may not be Australia. It could be an island, or another iceberg.' Ellen silently prayed that it was not. She could not bear much more of this dreadful journey — not least because it was becoming harder for her to keep her resolve and regard Richard as merely her employer. With each day that passed she was falling more deeply in love.

'Stay here with Mama. I will go and find out what's happening.'

She stumbled towards the cabin door and made her way through the deserted recreation area. Holding on to the doorframe she looked out into the deepening twilight. Sailors were swarming up the rigging but at another shout from aloft they paused in their work to look to the left. Ellen followed their gaze and at first could not see anything. But as the ship rose to the crest of another wave she saw a pinpoint of light on the horizon.

Impulsively she grabbed at the sleeve of a passing crewman. 'Is it land? Are we there at last?' she asked.

He shook her off and laughed, showing blackened broken teeth. 'That's the lighthouse at Cape Otway, Miss. We're still a long way from Sydney — that's if we get there at all in this weather. Best get back to your quarters, Miss.'

She stood for a moment, watching with mixed emotions the tiny glimmer that came and went as the ship ploughed on through the waves. Journey's end was in sight at last and she began to feel the excitement of adventure that she'd experienced at the start of the voyage. But deep down there was despair that their arrival would also see the end of her all too short friendship with Richard Gray, the handsome doctor who had stolen her heart.

She sighed and went slowly back to the cabin where Jessie had roused herself to light the lamp and Amelia was jumping about in excitement. 'Are we there yet? What did the man say?' she asked, clutching at Ellen's hand.

'There's a long way to go to Sydney but we are near the coast of Australia. Fetch the atlas and I'll show you.'

Ellen tried to explain that distances on a map were far different from real distances. And a good thing to, she thought, as she saw how narrow the strait between the Cape and King Island seemed. When Richard came in he reassured her. 'Captain Stark knows what he is about. He has given the order to heave to until daylight and then make our way through the straits.' He lowered his voice. 'There are dangerous reefs and in these heavy seas it would be folly to proceed.'

Jessie heard him and gasped, her hand to her mouth. Richard sat beside her and took her hand. 'Do not fear, my dear. As I said, we have a good captain and crew. Has he not brought us this far without mishap?'

Ellen smiled at his concern for his sister. But her heart was heavy as she wished she were the one whose hand he was stroking so tenderly. She was not given the chance to dwell on it, however, as Amelia claimed her attention.

'Show Uncle Richard the map, Ellen,' the little girl commanded. 'See,

Uncle, it is only a little way to Sydney and then I shall see my papa.'

He smiled and ruffled her curls. 'And what a great day that will be — but until then you will have to make do with your old uncle,' he said.

'And Ellen,' said Amelia. 'I've asked her to come and live with us when we get to our new house but she says she has her own house to go to.'

He looked up and caught Ellen's eye. 'Perhaps she will let us visit her there,' he said.

'Oh, yes, please, Ellen. Mama and I will come and take tea with you, but we will leave our card first, just like at home in England.'

'I don't think it will be quite like England,' Ellen said. 'Australia is a new country and they do things differently there. I think your mama will be too busy to come calling on me.'

Richard stood up. 'I must be on my rounds before lights out,' he said. At the door, he paused. 'You know I am staying on the ship. I have business in

England. But I intend to return to Australia. I hope you will allow me to call on you when I get back.'

While Ellen struggled for a suitable reply, Jessie said, 'I am sure Ellen will have settled into her new life by then. I do not think it would be appropriate . . . '

'That is for me to decide,' Richard snapped and left the cabin.

When he had gone Jessie turned to Ellen. 'I am sorry, my dear, but you must see there is no future in this friendship. I know they say things are different in the colony but surely the proprieties are still observed.' Her words were kind, but Ellen saw a hardness in the other woman's eyes.

An angry retort rose to Ellen's lips but she bit it back. 'You have no need to worry. As I said to Amelia, I have a family and work to go to. My sister's store is in a settlement outside Sydney, far from the sort of society you will be mixing with. And besides . . . '

'I am glad we understand one

another,' Jessie interrupted.

Ellen was glad to let the matter drop. She had almost blurted out that she was engaged to be married. But something made her hold back.

The *Caroline* got underway again at dawn, creeping through banks of swirling mist. The lighthouse at Cape Otway was far behind them and once again there was no sign of land. As the sun rose, the fog cleared and the ship picked up speed, the wind filling the sails. When Ellen went on deck, holding Amelia tightly by the hand, the passengers seemed brighter and less haggard than before.

Ellen lifted Amelia to the rail and pointed out a huge bird that skimmed the waves alongside the ship. The little girl laughed in delight. 'What's that smell, Ellen?' she asked.

Ellen breathed in a rich spicy scent, a refreshing change from the smell of stale clothing and unwashed bodies that she had become used to on board. 'It smells like flowers,' she said. 'I think it must mean we are near land.'

She pointed towards a band of low cloud on the horizon. 'It's over that way — Australia.'

As she descended the steps from the poop deck, holding tightly to Amelia's hand, she spied Millie and Joan chatting with a group of steerage passengers. Ignoring Jessie's instructions that her daughter was not to mix with 'those people', she stopped to speak to them. She had not seen her friends for a week, and despite Richard's reassurance, she had to see for herself that they were all right.

'Well, well, got time for us now, have yer,' Millie said.

'Don't, Mill. You're just jealous 'cause Ellen's been livin' it up without us,' said Joan.

'Not exactly living it up,' Ellen said, taking no notice of Millie's jibes. She was used to her by now and knew there was no malice in it. 'I've been kept busy with the little one's mama. She has been sick again.'

'So this is Amelia.' Joan bent down. 'Pleased to meet you, Miss. And what is your dolly's name?'

Amelia smiled shyly but responded to Joan's overtures. They were soon engaged in conversation, leaving Ellen and Millie to chat.

'I heard how you rescued the kiddie,' Millie said. 'Daft thing to do — you could have been drowned yourself.'

'I didn't have time to think,' Ellen said. 'Besides, you'd have done the same in my place.'

Millie gave a scornful laugh. 'Not likely.'

Joan looked up from her conversation with Amelia. 'Are you getting excited now we're nearly there?' she asked.

'Relieved, more like,' Ellen replied. 'I was beginning to think this voyage would go on for ever.'

'It's not over yet,' said Millie. 'Still, you must be looking forward to meeting your intended at last.'

'I'm more nervous than excited.'

'Not surprising. But surely you're a bit excited. A wedding . . . ' Joan's voice was dreamy. 'Wish it was me.'

'Your turn will come,' Millie said.

'And yours.'

'No fear. I'm not getting hooked up with some man who'll drink my money and leave me with a hoard of kids to bring up.'

'It doesn't have to be like that — if you meet the right man,' Ellen protested.

'And I supposed you think my brother's the right man,' a shrill voice interrupted.

Ellen swung round to face Jessie. Her hair was awry and her eyes were wild as she snatched Amelia away from the group of women. 'I have told you before — I will not have my chid consorting with these people.' She pulled the child towards her, despite the little girl's protests. 'Come, Amelia, back to the cabin.'

'But I want to stay with Ellen,' she said.

'Well, you cannot. Miss Campbell disobeyed my orders and is no longer in my employ.'

Ellen found her voice. 'I was never in your employ in the first place,' she said. 'And, as for your brother, you need have no fear. I am sure you will be pleased to hear that I am already engaged to be married.'

She turned away and, accompanied by her friends, descended to the steerage quarters. But not before she had seen the look on Richard's face as he came round the corner.

Ellen threw herself on to the bunk and burst into tears. Joan patted her shoulder and offered her a handkerchief. 'Don't let them upset you, love. They're not worth it — and after all you did for 'em too.'

Millie gave one of her scornful laughs. 'It's the doctor she's cryin' over — I knew you was sweet on him. Well, I warned yer, didn't I? Besides, what about the feller waitin' for you in Sydney?'

Ellen continued to sob and Joan glared at Millie. 'Leave her alone. Can't you see she's upset?'

'I'm all right.' Ellen blew her nose, sniffed and sat up. 'I'm just being silly that's all. Millie's right, I should have realised . . . '

'No, you're not being silly,' Joan said. 'You can't help falling in love. But what are you going to do about James?'

'What can I do? I've promised to marry him.'

Over the next few days Millie continued to make taunting comments prompted, Ellen suspected, by jealousy. She tried to ignore her but she had to acknowledge that the other girl was right — she had fallen in love with a dream.

One day, as she leaned on the ship's rail lost in thought, Millie couldn't resist another taunt. 'Still dreaming about the doc?'

'Don't be so unkind, Millie,' Joan said.

'Well, she must've known the doc

wasn't serious. And at least she's got a feller waitin' for her when we reach land. We should be so lucky. What's goin' to happen to us, eh?'

'We'll find work — they promised us, didn't they?' Joan said.

Ellen, preoccupied with her own troubles, hadn't given much thought to what would happen to her friends when they arrived. How selfish she had been. 'I thought you both had jobs waiting for you,' she said.

'Nothing's fixed,' Millie said. 'There's an agency which allocates positions to single women. Why should you care? You'll be all right.'

'Oh, Millie, don't be like that. Of course I care. Besides, I'm just as anxious as you are about what the future holds.'

'But you're getting married,' Joan said.

'I'm still nervous though.'

Millie gave a sarcastic laugh and Ellen shook her head. 'It's nothing to do with Doctor Gray. I would have been having second thoughts in any case. I don't know what I was thinking of, accepting a proposal from someone I don't know.'

'But your sister said he was a good man,' Joan said.

Ellen sighed. 'I suppose I'll have to trust her judgment and go through with it.' But her heart quailed at the thought.

As the ship drew nearer to Sydney, she began to wish that the end of the voyage, which she had longed for, would never come. She dreaded the coming meeting with James. How could she go through with the marriage feeling as she did? Despite knowing that she had no future with Richard, it was impossible to forget him, especially when she occasionally caught a glimpse of him going about his duties. Now though, instead of his warm smile, she encountered only cold glances and a swift turning away. Was he merely angry at what he would see as her deception? Or was he hurting as much as she was?

A few days later the Bass Strait with

its dangerous reefs was behind them and they were bearing north east up the coast of New South Wales. From time to time there were tantalising glimpses of land, towering cliffs that even from a distance looked hostile and unwelcoming.

The flowery scent was now mixed with a sharp medicinal smell which one of the sailors told her came from the leaves of the gum trees. 'You'll get used to it after a while and when you've been there a few weeks you won't even notice it at all.'

Ellen liked it — at least it was a fresh clean smell, far removed from what she'd had to endure in the hovel she'd had to call home for those months after her uncle's death. The scent of land told her that journey's end was near and she determined to make the best of it.

7

Four months to the day after leaving the port of London, the *Caroline* tied up at the quayside in Sydney harbour. The immigrants who had spent so long confined below decks in steerage, crowded towards the companionway in their eagerness to set foot on dry land once more. But Captain Stark had given orders that they must stay below until the first class passengers had disembarked and their luggage was unloaded.

At last, after what seemed like hours since that first cry of 'Landfall', they were allowed up into the fresh air. Ellen had gathered her belongings together and was sitting on the bunk. She clutched at her stomach which was now churning far worse than at any time during their perilous voyage. Now that the moment had come she was reluctant to move.

But, urged on by Millie and Joan who were eager to discover what exciting adventures awaited them, she picked up her belongings and followed them up on deck. Unlike her friends, she had no interest in the sights and sounds of the strange land.

As they reached the head of the gangway, Ellen felt a tug on her arm. 'There — isn't that woman waving at you?' Joan said.

'I'm not expecting to be met,' she replied. 'My sister lives outside the city and has given instructions how to get there.' She glanced to where her friend was pointing and her heart leapt.

It was Mary. Roused from her lethargy, she returned the wave vigorously, pushed past the last stragglers and rushed down on to the quay. She threw her arms round her sister and hugged as if she'd never let go.

Tears streaming down her face, the older woman finally pushed her away. 'Let me look at you.' She dabbed at her eyes. 'My little sister — I can't believe you're really here at last, safe and sound.'

'How did you know when to come?'

'The ship was late and I was beginning to worry. I needed to come to town to stock up and heard that the *Caroline* was due in very soon. So I stayed to welcome you.'

'I thought Patrick would be with you — and James. Are they minding the store?'

A shadow crossed Mary's face and Ellen clutched her arm. 'Nothing's happened to them?' she asked.

Mary shook her head angrily. 'They should have been here — but like most people in this place they've got gold fever. Gone off to the diggings, they have.'

Ellen couldn't help feeling relieved that the moment of coming face to face with James would be postponed for a little longer. But she could understand her sister's displeasure.

Mary took her carpetbag and one of

the bundles. 'We'd best be on our way — it's a two day journey,' she said. 'Come on, the cart's over here.'

'Wait — I must say goodbye to my friends,' Ellen said.

Millie and Joan were standing nearby, while a man with a clipboard read out names and allocated places for the new immigrants. Those without jobs already would be housed in hostels until accommodation and work could be found for them.

Ellen introduced them to Mary and wished them well in the future. She pressed a piece of paper into Joan's hand. 'If either of you ever need anything, that's where you'll find me. Keep in touch, won't you?' She gave them both a hug and with a lump in her throat turned to follow her sister.

Mary led her over to the horse and cart, where a boy with black curly hair stood holding the reins. Ellen stared curiously but when the boy smiled at her, showing white teeth in his dark skin, she couldn't help smiling back.

'This is Jonas,' Mary said. 'He lives at the mission but sometimes helps me in the store.'

The boy threw the luggage up on the cart and leapt up, taking the reins. As Ellen was about to follow she heard someone calling her name.

She turned and Amelia threw herself into her arms, sobbing. 'You were going away without saying goodbye.'

'I thought you had already gone,' she said, patting the little girl's back to soothe her. She looked over Amelia's shoulder and saw Jessie standing with Richard and another man. 'Is that your papa? I think he wants you to go now,' she said.

Amelia stopped crying and smiled. 'I knew he would be here when we got off the ship,' she said. 'Will you come and be introduced?' She tugged at Ellen's hand.

'I'm sorry. My sister is waiting for me.'

She gave the little girl another hug, stifling the lump in her throat. Their lives would take different paths from now on and Ellen knew she would miss the child. As she tried to disengage herself, a shadow fell across them. She looked up to see Richard standing there.

'Come, Amelia, Mama and Papa are waiting,' he said. 'Say goodbye to Miss Campbell.' His voice was stiff and formal as he turned to Ellen. 'As you know, I am returning to England. But I could not leave without thanking you for your help on the voyage. My sister asks me to convey her thanks too — and her good wishes for your forthcoming marriage.'

He held out his hand and Ellen shook it, hoping he would not detect its trembling. She managed to keep her voice steady as she replied, 'I am pleased to have been of assistance. I hope you have a safe journey.'

He took Amelia's hand and strode away.

'Goodbye, Ellen,' Amelia called.

Ellen raised a hand in farewell. But her eyes were too blurred with tears to see whether either of them waved back.

As the cart began its bumpy journey over the rutted streets, she scarcely noticed the noise and bustle as people and horse-drawn carts vied for space in the busy roads around the port. But gradually she began to take an interest in her surroundings as Mary pointed out the fine houses overlooking the harbour, the warehouses and wharves thronged with people.

On the outskirts of the city, gangs of former convicts were repairing the roads and digging foundations for the new buildings that were springing up everywhere. Despite herself she felt a twinge of excitement and she became even more determined to make a success of this new life, to forget the handsome doctor and his family and look to the future.

When her sister asked about her relationship with the little girl and her family, Ellen dismissed the subject, saying briefly, 'I nursed the mother when she was ill on the voyage.' She smiled and sat up straighter. 'Now, tell me about yourself — and the place we are going to. And are you happy in this life you have chosen?'

Mary laughed. 'One question at a time please.' But her radiant smile was answer enough. She put a hand over her stomach. 'The first thing I should tell you is that I am with child.'

Ellen hugged her sister once more. 'You must be thrilled — I know it is what you have wanted for a long time.'

A shadow crossed Mary's face as she thought of the two babies she had already lost. 'I am sure everything will be all right this time,' she said. 'But now you see why I am annoyed with Patrick for going off to the gold fields.'

'I don't blame you. He should be with you at this time. Was he aware of your condition when he left?'

Mary nodded. 'He did offer to stay but James persuaded him — even though I said you could arrive any day. His reply was that he hoped to make a fortune so that he would have something to offer you.'

Although Ellen was relieved at the inevitable delay to her marriage, she was angry too — more on her sister's behalf than her own. How could the brothers be so thoughtless as to go off into the wilderness leaving Mary to cope with a possibly dangerous pregnancy all alone?

Mary sensed her distress and laid a hand on her arm. 'I do not mind so much — now you are here,' she said. 'And I am sure Patrick would not have gone but for knowing I should have you beside me when the time comes.'

Ellen nodded sympathetically but she couldn't help wondering what would have happened to her sister if the ship had been delayed further or — even worse — had foundered in one of the fierce storms. But she said nothing, not wishing to distress her further.

Mary too, changed the subject, and began to tell her about the small settlement to the north of the city. In fact it was a rapidly growing town in its own right, set beside the River

Hawksbury. 'It is good land, once it is cleared. We can grow most of the crops we have in England — as well as some things I've never heard of. Then there is the timber which is needed for the new building. The loggers set up their camps along the river and float the trees downstream.'

'And what about the store? Who is in charge while you're away?'

'There is an old man — Billy. He was a stockman, got hurt when he was thrown from his horse. Now he lives at the pub across the road and helps Lizzie with the heavy work. Since the men left he's been helping me too.'

'Who's Lizzie?'

'She runs the pub. Goodness knows how she came to be out here living alone. But she's a good-hearted woman, works hard and keeps the men in order.' Mary laughed.

'Have you made any other friends?'

'There aren't many women in town and it's not like back home where you would meet people at church and such.

In fact we don't even have a church — just a travelling minister who holds services in the open.'

The cart lumbered along a track which Mary called a road but which was nothing like the roads Ellen was used to. She clutched the seat as her eyes darted everywhere trying to take in her strange surroundings.

They forded several streams which Mary told her were called creeks out here and as the city fell further behind, the virgin forest closed in around them. Occasionally the trees thinned out to reveal a cluster of buildings and a section of cleared land. The houses were low and timber built with wide verandas shaded by creepers. 'How pretty,' she said.

'Practical too,' Mary said. 'If you think it's hot now, wait a month or two. Then you'll see how we need every bit of shade we can get. The veranda also helps to keep the inside of the house cool.'

'Is your house like these?'

'It's similar, but of course most of the building is taken up by the shop. Our living quarters are upstairs.' Mary tried to describe the house and the settlement of Lawson's Creek and Ellen listened avidly. But she was growing tired and a little apprehensive.

They had been travelling for what seemed like hours and the sun was lowering behind the trees. Mary had said it was a two day journey and they were alone in the middle of what seemed like a never-ending forest with only the boy Jonas to protect them.

He had been concentrating on guiding the cart between the ruts in the road, but suddenly he turned and began to jabber excitedly. Ellen caught a few English words mixed in with the gibberish and gathered that he was telling them they'd reached their destination. He led the horse off the road stopping in front of a wooden house.

By now Ellen was too exhausted to take in any more but she appreciated the warmth of their welcome as Mary introduced her to the couple who greeted them. She had met the Murphys on the voyage out and on her rare excursions to the city she always broke the journey here.

The next day they resumed their trek, starting out early in the cool of the morning. After hours of plodding progress along the convict built road Ellen was beginning to feel as she had on the ship — that she had entered another world which would go on forever.

8

To her surprise, Ellen soon settled into life at Lawson's Creek stores. The shop was a long low building fronted by a veranda which gave on to a wide rutted road. Behind were the storerooms and across a dusty yard, the stable where the horse and cart were kept and where Jonas slept.

Across the road was the pub owned by Mary's friend, Lizzie, where thirsty stockmen gathered to recover from their arduous work in the heat and dirt. The wide main street was lined with wooden buildings — a livery stable, a blacksmith's forge and a huddle of single-storey houses shaded by gum trees.

'But they'll come.' Mary told her. 'The town is growing all the time.'

With the men away at the gold fields, it was hard work for the women and

Ellen found there was little time to dwell on what had happened on the long voyage out. As she tried to cope with the heat of an Australian summer, everything that had gone before faded into a dream.

But, as the days passed she found she was enjoying the new life, despite the hard work. The people were friendly and Mary never stopped saying how delighted she was that her sister had joined her at last and how she could not manage without her.

The store sold everything from basic provisions to animal feed, tools, candles and paraffin for lamps. There were rolls of cloth for dressmaking and home furnishing, crockery and cutlery.

Occasionally Jonas would disappear and this time he'd been gone for several days.

'Where's he gone?' Ellen asked.

'Gone walkabout,' Mary replied, laughing at Ellen's puzzled expression. 'That's what they call it. They go off into the bush for days, sometimes weeks, some kind of tribal ritual I think.'

'He works hard when he is here, though,' Ellen said.

Mary stretched and rubbed her back. 'Wish he was here at the moment. There's so much to do. I really don't understand it — he's fed and clothed, has somewhere comfortable to sleep. Why go wandering off out there . . . ' She waved a hand towards the edge of town and the wilderness beyond.

'Perhaps he misses his old way of life,' Ellen said. 'Anyway, it's the men who should be here. I think it's very thoughtless of Patrick to go off and leave you to cope on your own. You shouldn't be lifting this heavy stuff. I'll pop over and see if Billy's around.'

Ellen was still annoyed with her brother-in-law — and with James. What sort of man went off into the wilderness only days before his intended bride was expected — even if it was to make a fortune? As for leaving a pregnant wife to cope alone, it was unforgivable. She

130

could not help thinking that Richard Gray would not have been so thoughtless.

As the days passed, the novelty of her surroundings wore off. She didn't mind the heat or the hard work. But she was becoming increasingly concerned about her sister as her pregnancy advanced. There had been no word of the Turner brothers and Ellen's anger with them intensified as Mary constantly worried that something might have happened to them.

The men who searched for gold had not only the hardships of the diggings to contend with but the fear of being attacked and robbed when they did eventually strike lucky. Sometimes a horseman would ride into town with news from afar but it was never what the sisters wanted to hear.

Mary was nearing her time and she needed her husband with her. She seemed tired all the time and Ellen worried that something would go wrong. Suppose she had to cope with the birth on her own? 'Have you made arrangements — is there a midwife or a doctor?' she asked anxiously.

'There's no doctor in town. But Lizzie has promised to help,' Mary said.

Ellen was relieved. She'd had visions of having to deliver the baby herself. But Lizzie, despite her rough language and careless manner, was a sensible woman with a warm sense of humour.

Mary's baby was born in the small hours of a humid airless morning in January, the hottest month of the year. Her labour was long and difficult, her cries of pain punctuated with alternately cursing Patrick and begging him to return.

Ellen could do little but hold her sister's hand and pray while Lizzie bustled around doing her best to ease the passage of the tiny new life into the world. At last it was over and Lizzie handed the squalling baby to Ellen. 'A fine boy,' she said, nodding with satisfaction. 'You clean him up while I see to your sister.'

Ellen thought her nephew looked more like a skinned rabbit than a fine boy, although he certainly had a good pair of lungs on him. She wrapped him in a piece of blanket and took him into a corner of the room where a basin of warm water had been prepared. As she tenderly washed the baby, wiping the mucus from his nose and mouth, a wave of love washed over her. She dried him and wrapped him up again so that only his screwed up face and a tuft of dark hair was showing.

Lizzie had finished tending to Mary and she gestured Ellen to bring the child over to the bed. 'Here he is, my duck,' she said.

Mary opened her eyes and held out her arms, her smile wiping the lines of pain and exhaustion from her face. She cradled the baby in her arms and looked up at Ellen. 'I'm going to call him Henry after our father,' she said.

Mary did not recover from the birth. Despite Lizzie's best efforts, she could not stop the bleeding. Long after she had slipped away, Ellen sat holding her sister's hand, too numb to cry.

Little Henry's weak cry roused her and she picked him up, pacing the floor as she wondered what to do. In their former life it would have been easy to find a wet-nurse for the baby. But out here . . . Oh, why had she come to this god-forsaken place? Looking down into the screwed-up face of her tiny nephew gave her the answer. She would care for him as if he were her own.

Lizzie touched her arm. 'I'll send someone to fetch the minister in the morning,' she said.

Ellen nodded. There was a non-conformist chapel in the next town and, in the absence of a priest, the minister would have to do. She was more concerned with the living at this moment. 'What about the baby? How are we going to feed him?' she asked.

'Don't worry, my duck. I'll show you what to do.' Lizzie led her through to the kitchen and made her sit at the scrubbed table in the middle of the room. The baby continued to cry and Ellen jiggled him helplessly in her arms as Lizzie put some milk to warm on the stove.

'You watch that. I won't be a minute.' Lizzie disappeared but soon returned carrying a beer bottle. She laughed at Ellen's expression. 'Don't worry — I've washed it out.' She poured the milk into the bottle then stuffed a piece of clean rag into the neck. 'There, stick that in his mouth.'

Within seconds the baby's pitiful cries had given way to a contented sucking.

Ellen did her best but she began to find caring for the baby while trying to run the store was too big a task for one person. Billy helped when Lizzie could spare him, but this was a busy period. Everyone wanted to get their stock moved before the rainy season made the roads impassable and almost every day now the little town was filled with the shouts of the stockmen and the lowing of cattle. In the evenings the men crowded into the pub where they sang and gambled into the night.

Their presence was good for business but Ellen knew she needed help. Jonas had gone walkabout yet again and Billy had not yet appeared. Today she had opened up the store by herself, wiping down the counters with a damp cloth to try and get rid of the ever-present dust. She swept the floor, pushing the dirt out on to the veranda, and leaned on her broom to catch her breath.

Across the wide street, Lizzie was doing the same thing. 'How's the little feller?' she called.

Ellen threw down her broom and crossed the road. 'Thanks to you, he's doing well.'

'I knew that goat's milk would do the trick,' she said. 'Thank goodness I remembered Mrs Kennedy had a nanny goat.'

Henry had not thrived on the cow's milk they had been giving him and Ellen had been worried that he would not survive until Lizzie had found the solution. She ran a hand across her sweating forehead and brushed automatically at the flies which always seemed to hover just out of reach.

'He might be doing all right — but what about you? No sign of those Turner boys yet?' Lizzie looked at her in concern.

'I've almost given up on them. But I can't go on like this,' Ellen said. 'When they do finally get here, I'm going to give them such a tongue-lashing.'

'Let's hope they've struck rich,' Lizzie said.

'I don't really care — I just wish Patrick would come back and take responsibility for his son.' She sighed. 'Sometimes, I wish I'd stayed in London.'

Lizzie snorted. 'I wouldn't go back — not for a fortune in gold.' She touched Ellen's arm. 'It's a good life out here if you make up your mind to it. But it's not for everyone. Maybe you'd be better off in the city.'

'I can't leave the store — not till I get

some news of Patrick at least.'

The idea of going to Sydney and getting a job was appealing. She had friends there and she knew there was plenty of work available. But she couldn't leave little Henry and there was no way she could take him with her.

A few days later Billy was unloading some sacks from a wagon when he slipped. The fall reawakened his old injury and he was laid up for days. Then Jonas went off on one of his walkabouts.

'I'm going to have to close the store,' Ellen said when, as usual at the end of each exhausting day, she and Lizzie sat on the veranda with a drink, gazing at the stars and enjoying the rest. 'I don't know how you manage. It's just too much . . . '

'Well, I don't have a baby to look after. But you're right. I didn't realise how much I relied on Billy.'

'How is he?'

'On the mend. But I don't think he'll

be fit for work for a while.'

'Isn't there anyone round who needs a job? Not that I can pay much . . . '

'Most of them would rather take their chances at the diggings than do an honest day's work,' Lizzie said.

'Still, we must do something.' Ellen was silent for a moment. An idea that has been lingering in her minds for some time took shape. 'I could go to Sydney — find someone to work for us. I know a couple of people who might be willing to come out here. And if they've already got jobs, there are agencies who find work for new immigrants.'

'I'd be a bit wary of taking on a feller without knowing him,' Lizzie said.

'I was thinking more of a woman.'

'That's no good — I tried it. Had a pretty little thing working in the bar once, serving the drinks. The fellers loved it. But she fell for one of 'em, took off and got married just as I'd got her trained up nicely.'

'Just an idea,' Ellen said.

'And if you did go, what about young Henry — and the shop?'

'I'd take him with me of course. And I'll close the store, unless Jonas comes back.'

'You can't leave that feller in charge,' Lizzie protested.

'No, you'd be in charge, Lizzie — if you don't mind. After all, anyone who comes into town for supplies comes to you as well. You could take their money, make sure they pay for whatever goods they take. I'll only be gone a few days — a week at the most.'

Ellen warmed to the idea. She was sure if she managed to track down Millie and Joan, she could persuade them to join her in Lawson's Creek. It would be so good to have her friends nearby.

It took some time to persuade her, but eventually Lizzie gave in. It helped that Billy was recovering from his accident and was now able to hobble around a little with the aid of a stick. He agreed to mind the store, although he wouldn't be able to do the heavy work.

Excitedly, Ellen began to plan her trip to the city, ignoring Lizzie's warnings about the dangers of travelling alone. The night before she was due to leave, she found it hard to sleep. But it was not apprehension about the forthcoming journey that weighed on her mind. It was the little thrill of anticipation that, even if he had not yet returned to Australia, she might gain news of Richard Gray.

She was still officially engaged to be married and she knew she should not be thinking of him at all. But as far as she was concerned, James Turner had forfeited their engagement by his thoughtless behaviour. He had not even left a note for her and in all these months there had been no word of him or his brother.

9

Ellen broke her journey at the Murphys' farmstead as she had almost a year before with her sister. They were as kind and welcoming as they'd been on her previous visit, but talking to them about Mary's death was hard. It was a relief when it was time to say goodbye and start off for the city. She left in the cool of early morning, promising to stay over again on her return.

Mrs Murphy had given her the address of a boarding house where she could lodge during her stay in Sydney.

The boarding house was in a street not far from the harbour, the perfect place to start her search. The proprietor was a tall thin woman called Mrs Johnson, who frowned and looked disapproving when she saw that Ellen was alone. But her thin lips curved into a smile when Ellen mentioned the

Murphys and, when she saw little Henry, her welcome was effusive.

'I'm sure you'll find plenty of people willing to come and work for you. People are always looking for jobs,' she said when Ellen explained her reasons for coming to the city.

She had no idea where to start her search for her friends. Surely there was some sort of immigration office where she could ask for help? But by the third day, she was despairing of finding news of them and was almost resigned to returning to Lawson's creek with a stranger.

She had left Henry with Mrs Johnson, the landlady of the boarding house, and decided to have one last try before going to the employment agency she had recommended and interviewing a couple of applicants.

The office faced on to the waterfront and, among the ships waiting to tie up at the wharf, Ellen spied the *Caroline*. Her heart started thumping and she took a step forward, her lips forming the name 'Richard'. Foolish girl, she admonished herself. He would not be on board. He had told her he was giving up his work as ship's surgeon to concentrate on his research work. He would not have returned to Australian so soon.

She turned away and bumped into someone. For a moment, the gaudy clothes and painted face prevented her from recognising the other woman. It wasn't until the eyes widened and a smile lit up her face that she realised it was Millie.

'Ellen, what you doing down here? I thought I'd never see you again.' She grabbed Ellen's hand. 'No ring, I see. So you didn't marry your feller after all?' She gave a screech of laughter. 'Knew you wouldn't — too stuck on the doc — not that it did you any good. So what's with you then?'

'Millie, it's lovely to see you.' Ellen tried to hide her shock. It was obvious her friend had gone back to her old life. What had happened to her vows to lead a respectable life in the new country?

'I know what you're thinking but . . . ' Millie's voice trailed away.

'I'm sorry. I'm not judging you, truly. What happened — and what about Joan?'

'She fell on her feet, working as a maid in some posh house.' Millie sniffed. 'I picked the wrong place to work — so-called gentleman . . . '

'Couldn't you have told the agency — found another job?'

'Who'd believe me, eh? No, the missus refused to give me a reference. So here I am — back on the game.' She smiled and straightened her shoulders. 'And what about yourself? Don't tell me things didn't work out for you either?'

Ellen took the other woman's arm. 'It's a long story. Let's go and get a bite to eat and I'll tell you all about it.'

They found an eating house facing the water, with a view of the harbour and the small boats plying between the quayside and the ships out in the bay.

'This is a good place,' Millie said.

'It's cheap, clean too — and the food's not bad.'

Settled at a table by the window with bowls of thick savoury stew in front of them, Ellen told her friend all that had happened since they'd last met.

'I'm sorry about your sister. What's going to happen to the baby?'

'I'll care for him like he's my own. It's the least I can do.'

'What will James say to that when he gets back — and the kid's father?'

'I don't care about James — I only want what's right. I promised Mary I'd look after little Henry. When Patrick returns we'll sort something out.'

'You should leave Lawson's Creek — come to Sydney.'

'I can't get a job while I've got the baby. Besides, I need to keep the store going — it's Henry's inheritance, if anything happens to his father too.'

'Hadn't thought of that,' Millie said.

'That's why I'm here. I need help and I wondered if you and Joan would like to come and work for me. Of course, when the men turn up — if they ever do — things could change. But I'd love to have you both with me.'

'It's tempting,' Millie said.

'What about Joan? Is she too settled do you think?'

'She seems happy enough. I sometimes see her on her day off — that's tomorrow. We could ask her.

They finished their meal and Ellen paid the bill. Outside, Millie gave her a hug. 'See you here tomorrow then — same time.'

Ellen watched as her friend walked quickly away, passing two men on the quayside, deep in conversation. The one facing her was Captain Stark and she caught her breath as the other took his hat off and gave a little bow.

The bright sun gleaming on golden hair and for a moment she was sure it was Richard. It's just because he's on my mind so much, she told herself. It was hard to walk away without making sure. But if it was him, what would she say to him after all these months?

She decided to take Henry with her when she went to meet her friends the next day. He was getting heavy and by the time she reached the restaurant she was glad to sit down. She propped him in a chair next to her, tying him on with her shawl so that he didn't fall. At six months he was very lively, sitting up on his own, smiling and gurgling at everyone. How proud Mary would have been, Ellen thought, stroking his dark curly head.

The door opened and Joan and Millie entered. Joan rushed over and enfolded Ellen in a hug. 'I couldn't believe it when Millie said . . . Oh, it's good to see you. How are you? And this little feller . . . Oh, he's sweet . . . ' The words tumbled out without giving Ellen the chance to answer.

Millie too, was exclaiming over the baby and Ellen smiled indulgently. She hadn't thought her friends had much time for children. But who could help loving Henry with his rosy cheeks and gummy smile?

They sat down at last and Millie beckoned the waiter over and gave their order. Ellen noticed that Millie was more soberly dressed today and had not used quite so much make-up. It was a sign that despite her defiant air, she cared what Ellen thought and, maybe was considering taking up the offer of employment. Joan too, seemed eager to hear about Lawson's Creek and life in the small community.

They had their heads together, neglecting their food and talking animatedly, pausing occasionally to feed titbits to the baby. He seemed content, smiling round at them and banging a spoon on the table to crows of delight.

Ellen was sure that Joan was ready to give in her notice and come to Lawson's Creek with her but Millie couldn't make up her mind. She stood up and began to untangle the baby from her shawl. 'I'll be at the boarding house till tomorrow — I can't stay any longer. I've been gone too long already. If you're not there by noon, I'll tell the agency to send someone.'

While they had been talking, the restaurant had become noisy and smoky, filling up with workers coming in for their noon meal. Two men who had been sitting on stools at the bar, stood up to take the table the women were vacating.

Ellen, her eyes blurred with tears as she said goodbye to her friends, hardly noticed them. 'I do hope you decide to come. I've missed you both,' she said.

'I'll be there,' Joan promised. 'And I'll talk her into it.' She gave Millie's arm a playful smack. Millie laughed, but her eyes were on the men. One of them had sat down, but the other was holding on to the back of his chair, staring at them.

As Ellen turned away she found herself looking into Richard's shocked face. She took a step forward, murmuring his name. He glanced down at the bundle in her arms and stumbled backwards, his face draining of colour. Without a word he walked away, ignoring his friend's protests. Ellen followed but stopped abruptly as the door banged shut, leaving her staring.

Joan and Millie tried to console her.

'It was just the shock of seeing you with a baby,' Joan said. 'He probably thinks you're happily married by now.'

'Still, he could have spoken. I wanted to ask how Amelia and Mrs Arnold are,' Ellen said, surprised at how steady her voice was. She had recovered her composure and was trying to pretend the incident had meant nothing to her.

Her friends were not deceived however. But for once Millie did not make one of her sarcastic comments.

Ellen went back to the boarding house and put Henry down for an afternoon nap while she packed her things for the journey back to Lawson's Creek — home as she must now think of it. The encounter with Richard had left her more shaken than she cared to admit.

The next day, as she loaded up the cart, she decided it would be a long time before she came to the city again. She couldn't face another encounter like yesterday's. Lawson's Creek was where she belonged now — and as soon as James returned, she was determined to marry him and settle down to running the store and raising a family of her own. She really didn't care whether or not he had found any gold.

She was not surprised when Joan appeared at the boarding house without Millie. She hadn't really expected to see her. 'It's a shame she's gone back to her old life, but it's her decision,' she told Joan. 'I only hope she remembers us if she ever needs a friend.'

'That's what I told her,' Joan said.

'What did your mistress say about you leaving without notice?' Ellen said, changing the subject.

'Refused to pay what she owed me and took back the two dresses she gave me,' Joan said. 'Never mind, she was an old sourpuss anyway, although the work wasn't hard and the food was good.'

They made a little nest of blankets in

the back of the cart for Henry and, after saying goodbye to Mrs Johnson, set off on their long journey. On the way, Ellen told her friend more about the Murphys, Lizzie, old Bill and the aboriginal boy Jonas.

Joan smiled at her. 'And you're really happy out here?' she asked.

'It's not a bad life, bit hard sometimes, but no worse than back in the old country.'

'I thought you'd be married with your own baby by now,' Joan said.

'Well, it's obvious James wasn't serious about wanting to settle down with a wife, since he went off just when I was due to arrive.'

'And there's been no word at all?'

'None. I'm starting to get worried.' Ellen shook her head. 'Oh, not about James — I really don't care one way or the other. But Patrick doesn't even know his wife's dead and that he has a son. You'd think he would at least have written for news.'

Joan was silent for a while as the cart

rattled along. Gazing round her at the strange countryside, she said. 'I like this. You really can tell you're in a different country. My mistress wanted everything to be like back home — she even tried to get English flowers to grow in her garden.'

Ellen smiled. 'I suppose you can't blame her — if she only came out to please her husband, she's probably homesick. But we chose to come, so I think we should — not exactly forget old England — but try to be Australian, if you see what I mean.'

When they forded the creek and drove up the wide main street, Ellen spotted Lizzie on her veranda.

The older woman waved and ran down the steps to greet her. 'Thank God you're back safe,' she said. 'I was starting to worry.'

'Is everything all right?' Ellen asked.

'No worries. Billy's kept it all going and Jonas is back.'

'No word of my brother-in-law?'

Lizzie shook her head. 'Either they've

struck it rich and they're living it up in Melbourne, or . . . '

'Patrick wouldn't do that. Something must have happened.'

'You can't be sure of that. Give them a bit more time before you start worrying.' Lizzie turned to Joan who was still sitting up on the cart, looking about her. 'Who's this then — the new help? Looks a bit skinny for heavy work.'

Ellen gave Joan a hand down from the cart and introduced her. 'Don't take any notice of Lizzie, she speaks her mind but she can take it too.'

Joan grinned. 'I'm stronger than I look.'

Lizzie laughed. 'I'm just glad Ellen's got someone to help. What about the other one?'

'Millie decided she was better off in Sydney,' Ellen said. 'We'll manage. But if the men don't get back soon, I'll contact the agency and ask for a man.' She blushed when both Joan and Lizzie started to laugh.

It was a joy to have Joan for company, although Ellen still missed her sister badly. And she could not quite rid herself of the feeling that she should have been able to do something for Mary, despite Lizzie's reassurance. She dreaded the thought of Patrick's return when she would have to break the news of his wife's death.

She had been back from Sydney for two weeks and she and Joan had settled into a routine with the help of Bill and Jonas. Bill had recovered from his fall, although he still walked with a limp. But his wiry strength was invaluable when there was any heavy work to be done.

The baby took up a lot of their time now as he had started to crawl about and showed a lively interest in everything around him. He needed watching all the time.

'He seems contented enough,' Joan said, watching him as he played with a pile of wood blocks. The two women were sitting on the veranda as they did most days during the heat of the afternoon. They sipped cool drinks, waving away the flies while they chatted idly.

'He's growing so fast. It's a pity his father can't see him. He'll be walking and talking soon.'

'Have you decided what you're going to do about James?' Joan asked.

Ellen sighed and gazed up the road to where a group of horsemen had just ridden in to town. 'Looks like work for us,' she said, starting to rise from her chair, glad of an excuse not to answer Joan's question. Most visitors to Lawson's Creek were here to stock up on supplies.

'Stay there. They're bound to want a drink first, riding in this heat. Let Lizzie deal with them,' Joan said.

Ellen sank back in her chair, smiling as Henry crawled towards her and grabbed at her skirt. She pulled him up, helping him to balance on unsteady legs, laughing as he tried to stand alone, falling on his bottom with a bump.

Before he could start to cry, she swept him up and kissed him.

The strangers were forgotten as she played with her nephew, until she heard footsteps on the veranda and a shadow fell across her. She looked up to see a man smiling down at her and it was some moments before she recognised her brother-in-law. His normally mousy hair was bleached by the sun and his tired face was lined and burnt from long hours spent outdoors.

'Patrick, you're back at last,' she exclaimed, jumping up.

'So — you arrived safely then?' He smiled and reached out a hand to touch his son's cheek. 'I knew it would be a boy,' he said. Then, glancing round, 'Where's Mary? Is she resting?'

10

Ellen's expression must have told Patrick what had happened. Before she could speak, his face paled beneath the dark sunburn and he sat down quickly, dropping his head in his hands. 'I knew I shouldn't have left her,' he said.

No, you shouldn't, Ellen thought. But she touched his arm and said, 'You weren't to know.'

He leaned forward to take the baby from Ellen, holding him close and kissing the rosy cheek. 'Tell me what happened — everything. Were you here when she . . . ?'

Joan went inside, leaving them to talk. When she had finished the long story, she hesitated, reluctant to ask about his brother. He looked across the road to the pub. 'James went for a drink. He's a bit nervous about meeting you.'

Ellen summoned a smile. 'He's not the only one.'

'So — how do you like it out here then?'

'It takes some getting used to. But it's starting to feel like home.' She followed Patrick's gaze. 'Does he really want to marry me?' she asked.

'I don't know. He doesn't say much. It was Mary's idea really. She was worried about you. Thought James would be a good match.'

He was only saying what Ellen had thought — it wasn't the first time her sister had tried match-making.

While Joan prepared a meal, she stayed on the veranda talking to Patrick and watching him getting to know his son. As they chatted she kept her eyes on the pub door, tensing every time it swung open.

When she had finished telling Patrick about the long voyage, she hesitated, unwilling to ask about his experiences at the gold diggings — he would have said if they'd had any luck. She could tell from his defeated expression that it had been a waste of time. She didn't understand this lust for riches when they already had a good business and enough to live on.

He seemed to read her thoughts. 'I wanted to give Mary more. She worked so hard, but I knew she wasn't very strong. If I'd struck rich she wouldn't have had to work so hard.'

'She didn't feel that way,' Ellen said. 'Was it your idea to go?'

'Yes. Well, James brought it up. We'd been talking to some prospectors in the pub and got excited about it. Before we knew it, we'd agreed to join a group going out the diggings. You know how it is.' His head dropped into his hands again. 'I shouldn't have gone.'

Someone came out of the pub and began to stroll across the street. He was so like his brother that Ellen knew it must be James and she tensed. By now she had worked herself up to a pitch of indignation. Useless to tell herself he was probably as nervous as she was.

Surely it was better to get the introduction over with?

He came up the steps and paused, glancing about him and twisting his hat in his hands. As she stood up, the door behind her opened and Joan came out. 'Dinner's ready,' she said, bending to pick Henry up. James took a step towards her, a smile lighting up his face. 'You must be Ellen,' he said.

Joan shook her head and Patrick slapped his brother on the back. 'You've been drinking, mate. This is Ellen.'

James looked confused. 'Where's Mary then?'

There was a moment's embarrassed silence, then they all began talking at once. Eventually, the misunderstanding was cleared up and they went into the house for their meal.

As they ate, Ellen studied James, trying to hide her distaste. She hoped he did not make a habit of drinking so much. Joan didn't seem to mind though. They seemed to be getting on well and hardly seemed to notice that neither she nor Patrick said very much during the meal.

She pushed her chair back and stood up. 'I think I heard Henry crying,' she said, and left the room. When she came back they were all outside on the veranda, enjoying the cool breeze that had sprung up. Patrick had lit his pipe and James was smoking a cigar, leaning against the railing and gazing down the street. Joan looked up, smiling. 'They've been telling me all about their adventures in the outback,' she said.

Patrick looked at his brother. 'I did not find it such an adventure,' he said. 'I was ready to give up months ago. But James kept saying 'one more day' — and I allowed myself to be persuaded.' His voice was bitter and he turned his head away. When he looked back at Ellen she could see that he had made a conscious effort to hide his feelings. 'Is my son all right?' he asked.

'He's sleeping now.' She sat down next to Joan. 'So, I take it you won't be going off on any more 'adventures' then?' she said.

Before he could reply, James said, 'There's too many going out now — there's going to be trouble there for sure. Besides, I have a reason for staying now.'

Ellen looked up with a smile, then looked quickly away as she saw that his eyes were on Joan. Had he forgotten he was supposed to be engaged to her? She was about to make a sharp comment when Patrick said, 'There's nothing to keep me here.' He stood up abruptly and went indoors.

James pushed himself off from the railing and ground the remains of his cigar out under his boot. 'Well, ladies, I'll bid you goodnight. I'm sleeping over the way.' He grinned. 'Can't spend the night under the same roof as my fiancée, can I?'

When he had gone, Joan glanced at her friend. 'Well, what did you think? He seems nice enough.'

'You might think so but, since he

hardly spoke to me all evening, I've not had a chance to form an opinion,' Ellen said. 'Besides, I'm more worried about Patrick at the moment. I didn't like his comment about having nothing to keep him here — he has a son after all.'

'He was thinking about Mary,' Joan said. 'The poor man has hardly had a chance to get used to the fact that his wife has died.'

Ellen realised how harshly she had judged him when she followed her brother-in-law indoors and found him leaning over little Henry's cot, tears pouring down his cheeks.

Tears rose in her own eyes. She still missed Mary so much. Suddenly it all seemed too much for her to bear and, instead of trying to comfort Patrick, she crept silently away to her own bed. Once there, sleep was a long time coming as she thought about her life which at the start of the voyage from England had held such promise.

Now here she was, trying to be mother to another woman's child, running another man's business, while at the same time trying to cope with her own confused feelings about the two men in her life. Of one thing she was quite sure though — she could not marry James. The only problem was finding an honourable way to break her promise.

11

Little Henry was teething and for the past week Ellen had got up several times a night to soothe him, trying not to disturb Joan in the next room, or Patrick asleep on the sofa downstairs. Much as she loved her nephew, the disturbed nights were taking their toll and she wished for once that someone else would take the responsibility.

Patrick could hardly bear to look at the child. He reminded him too much of Mary, he said when Ellen remonstrated with him.

Tonight Henry seemed more fretful than usual and she wondered if it was just his teeth bothering him. If he still seemed fractious the next day she would ask advice from one of the farmer's wives who sometimes came into the store.

She stretched out a hand to smooth

his hair and he clutched at her finger. Poor little mite — no mother and even his father did not seem to have much time for him.

It was true the brothers both worked hard. The town was growing daily and they had plans to expand so there was plenty to keep them all busy. There was little time to talk during the day and by nightfall they were all ready for their beds.

After their evening meal, James would depart across the road to his lodgings. Not a word about their engagement had been spoken and, although Ellen knew she should tackle him about it, she was reluctant to raise the subject. Suppose he felt he should honour their agreement? So far she had managed to avoid being alone with him. But it couldn't be put off forever.

Knowing there was no possibility of a future with Richard, she had been prepared to go through with marriage to James. He was pleasant enough and she was sure she could have made him happy. But that was before she had seen the way he and Joan had looked at each other. Perhaps it had been a mistake to ask Joan to come to Lawson's Creek. But how would she manage without her now?

Dawn was breaking and it seemed pointless to go back to bed. Besides, she would never sleep with all these thoughts churning about in her head. As she passed the living-room she glanced through the open door to see that Patrick was still asleep. It had seemed sensible while he was away for Ellen to move into Mary's room with the baby but she had offered to go in with Joan when he came back. But he said he couldn't bear it with Mary gone, and since his return had bunked down on the sofa.

Ellen sighed as the smell of booze reached her nostrils. Patrick had been drinking more lately and she could understand that it helped in is grief. But this situation could not go on. He was leaving more of the work to James and neglecting his son into the bargain.

On impulse she strode into the room and shook his shoulder. 'Time you were getting up,' she said.

'Oh, leave me be, woman. It's hardly light yet.' He snorted and turned over, pulling the blanket over his face.

Disgusted, she turned away and went into the kitchen. As she coaxed the stove into life and started preparing breakfast, she allowed herself to think of the future. Even if she married James, things would probably not change much. She'd still be keeping house for them all and bringing up her nephew. And all the time, she would be thinking of Richard. No matter how hard she tried, she could not forget him.

She should leave here, go to one of the cities — not Sydney, where she ran the risk of encountering him or his sister. There was plenty of work in Melbourne or Adelaide. She could make a completely new life for herself — and in the process leave the way clear for Joan and James to find happiness together. But she couldn't just leave. She owed James an explanation.

As if she had conjured him up, the screen door banged open and he came in. 'Ah, coffee,' he said, going over to the stove and helping himself. He leaned against the dresser, watching as Ellen fried bacon and eggs. 'Where's that brother of mine? Not still in bed surely?'

'He didn't sleep well. The baby was crying all night.' Ellen didn't know why she was defending him.

'I bet you were the one who got up to him, though. I'll go and rouse him out. There's a delivery due today.' He moved towards the kitchen door, shouting. 'Come on, Patrick, you lazy beggar.'

Impulsively, Ellen laid a hand on his arm. 'Don't make him yet. You and I have things to discuss.'

He looked down, studying his boots and coughed. 'Well, er — plenty of time,' he mumbled.

'No, there's not. I came out here at my sister's request, it's true. But you know there was another reason . . . '

She turned back to the stove, pretended to be absorbed in turning over the bacon in the pan. It was up to him to speak, after all.

The lengthening silence was broken by another cough. 'Patrick is talking about going back to the diggings. I thought I might go too.'

Ellen wheeled round, pan in her hand. 'He means to abandon his child? And when was he going to inform me of his decision? Does he expect me to be both mother and father to the poor little mite?' She banged the pan down on the table. 'You can see to your own breakfast. I have had enough of being taken for granted.'

She ran out of the room, pushing past Joan as she came downstairs. She sank on to the stool in front of her dressing-table and wiped away her tears. 'I'm just tired,' she murmured, 'so tired.' It wasn't like her to lose her temper. But she'd had enough.

She'd looked after her uncle until he died, then there was the responsibility of taking care of Amelia on the ship, now she had someone else's child to look after. Why couldn't someone take care of her, she thought, as fresh tears rolled down her cheeks.

She remembered Richard's strong but gentle hands as he wrapped the blanket round her after she had rescued Amelia from drowning. But it was no use thinking of Richard. He was far away — whether in Sydney or London, it made no difference.

As she dried her tears once more it suddenly dawned on her what James had said. If Patrick left, he would go too. He had obviously changed his mind about marrying her but was to cowardly to say so. Her temper rose again and she made up her mind to tackle him this minute.

Before she left the room she peeped into Henry's cot. He had not stirred and she touched his cheek gently. At once she withdrew her hand as she felt the heat coming from his skin. His face was flushed and his hair was damp. She had left the window open to allow a cool breeze in but he was burning up. His clothes were soaked in perspiration and he was breathing raggedly.

As she snatched him out of his cot, she noticed a bright red rash on his neck and chest. She ran downstairs with him in her arms. There was still no sign of Patrick, but Joan and James were seated at the table, deep in conversation, the plates of bacon and eggs going cold in front of them.

Joan jumped up when Ellen came in. 'What is it?'

'The baby's ill. I don't know what to do.' Ellen sat down, clutching Henry to her, frantically trying to remember what Richard had told her about treating fevers. Get his temperature down, that's it, and liquid. 'Water,' she gasped, 'Fill his bottle with water and get me a wet rag.'

To her surprise it was James who rushed to help. Joan stood by the door. 'I'll go and fetch Lizzie, she'll know what to do.'

While they waited for Lizzie, Ellen tried to get the baby to suck at the bottle. But his feeble attempts only resulted in the liquid running down his chin.

'Try this,' James said, dipping a clean rag in water and trickling it into Henry's mouth.

Ellen began to calm down and she smiled gratefully at James. He patted her shoulder and said, 'I'll roust out that brother of mine. It's his kid after all.'

She could hear him still berating Patrick when Joan returned with Lizzie, who dropped to her knees beside Ellen and examined the child. 'It doesn't look like the normal teething rash. He needs a doctor,' she said.

'But Sydney's two days away.' Ellen could not voice the thought that two days might be too late.

Lizzie sighed. 'I did hear that a doctor's set up practice in Hawker's Bend. It's four hours ride but Jonas could get there quicker and fetch him back — that's if he's prepared to come.'

James had come back into the kitchen with Patrick shuffling behind him. 'It will be quicker to go there ourselves,' James. 'I'll go and hitch up the cart.'

Patrick, who had seemed only half awake, pulled himself together when he saw the grave faces. 'Is he . . . ?' He took a step forward. 'I thought it was just his teeth coming through.'

'We all thought that,' Ellen said. 'But it seems he has a fever.'

'We're taking him to the doctor in Hawker's Bend,' Lizzie said.

James came back. 'Are you ready?'

Patrick pushed James aside. 'I'll go. He's my son.'

Ellen nodded. 'All right. You can drive the cart.'

'Do you want me to come too?' James asked.

'No, you stay with Joan and open up the store. It will help to take her mind off things.' She climbed up into the cart and Lizzie passed the baby up to her. She smiled at James. 'You don't have to say anything — I understand,' she said.

He gave an embarrassed grin and scuffed his toe in the dust. 'I'm sorry, Ellen.'

Patrick took the reins and, as they were about to move off, Joan came running out with a hastily wrapped parcel. 'It's the bacon and some bread — a bottle of water too. You've had no breakfast.'

Ellen knew she would not be able to eat but she thanked her anyway. 'Take care of James while we're gone,' she said. It was her way of letting Joan know that she wasn't unhappy with the way things had worked out.

She looked down at the baby, still apparently sleeping peacefully. But it wasn't a normal sleep and Ellen's heart gave a lurch. Please, God, let the doctor be there and don't let us be too late, she prayed.

Patrick turned to her, remorse in his eyes. 'I should have realised he was ill,' he said.

'It's not your fault.'

He grunted and urged the horse to go a bit faster over the rutted track.

'Are you really going back to the gold fields?' Ellen asked.

'I can't stay here. My heart's not in the business without Mary.'

'James won't come with you,' Ellen warned. 'He wants to be with Joan. I've realised that for some time.

'He told me — but he didn't know how to break it to you. That's why he wanted to go away again.'

'I don't mind. I hope they'll be happy,' Ellen said.

'And what about you? I've been selfish, I know, expecting that you'll stay and look after Henry. I thought that with you and James running the store . . . '

'I haven't decided yet. But I'll stay of course, until . . . ' She looked down at Henry again and her voice broke. They both knew that it all depended on whether the baby survived this dreadful fever. To save speaking again, she wet the rag from the water bottle and gently

178

bathed Henry's face, dribbling a little water into his mouth. It was all she could do.

They rode in silence until the outlying farms of the settlement came into view. Hawker's Bend was a bigger town than Lawson's Creek, set on the banks of the main river. There were a few substantial houses, some with gardens, and the main street was lined with shops and small businesses. Carts and pony traps rattled along the centre of the road and there was the noise and bustle of people going about their business.

Patrick stopped the cart outside the largest store and enquired where the doctor could be found. They were directed to one of the big houses a little farther down the street.

The housekeeper answered his frantic hammering. 'Clinic's round the back,' she said, 'but Doctor's finished for the day.'

Ellen handed the baby to Patrick and jumped down, snatching him back as soon as her feet touched the ground.

Leaving him to hitch the horse to a railing, she ran around the side of the house towards a small outbuilding.

As the door opened and a man came out and she stopped abruptly, feeling the blood drain from her face.

'What's the trouble?' Richard Gray asked, reaching for the child. Then he stopped too as recognition dawned. 'Ellen, my dear. Come in. Let me look at him.'

He led her into a large airy room and made her sit down. He laid Henry on a high bed and started to remove his clothing. 'How long has he been ill? When did you notice this rash?'

Ellen could not answer and Patrick, who had followed her into the room, said, 'We thought it were his teeth. He's been crying a lot at night.'

'Yes, there is sometimes a rash when teeth are coming though. But you did right to bring him to me.' He continued his examination, gently exploring the tiny body, looking into his eyes, probing his ears.

When he had finished he smiled reassuringly. 'Well, it's not measles, thank the Lord.' He tapped his chin. 'It could be some sort of milk fever. Have you been feeling well yourself, Ellen? No difficulties in feeding?'

Ellen shook her head, bewildered. As she realised what he meant, a slow blush suffused her face. He must still be under the impression that the baby was hers.

'No matter,' he said hastily, before she could reply. 'These fevers are quite common in children. You must stay here for a day or two so that I can keep an eye on him. Don't worry — if we can keep his temperature down, he will recover. But he needs careful nursing.' He turned to Patrick. 'I suggest you take a room at the hotel across the road. Your wife looks exhausted. Leave the baby here. My housekeeper will look after him and I will call you if there is any change.'

Ellen had been replacing Henry's clothing and she looked up now, a protest on her lips. Surely he had noticed that she wore no wedding ring?

But Patrick spoke first. 'Thank you, Doctor,' he said. 'But Ellen isn't . . . '

Richard didn't let him finish. He turned to Ellen. 'I know you would like to stay with the child. But you need to rest.' He smiled, his tender, heart-warming smile — not the bitter twist of the lips that she remembered from their last encounter. 'Go on — I'll call you if necessary.'

Patrick took her arm and led her outside. 'He's right. You need to sleep — and I need a drink.'

Ellen was too tired and confused to argue. She allowed herself to be led up to the room, leaving Patrick in the bar. She lay down on the bed, but the shock of seeing Richard again and the realisation that her feelings had not changed would not allow her to sleep.

His attitude, after that first jolt of recognition, had been of acceptance but she could not allow him to go on thinking that she was married with a child. Besides, she should stay with Henry. After all, she was the only mother he had now.

She swung her legs off the bed and stood up, feeling dizzy. After splashing her face with cold water from the jug on the washstand, she felt a little better and she made her way downstairs. Patrick was still at the bar slumped over a tankard of ale.

Ignoring him, she crossed the street to the doctor's house. Richard's housekeeper was at Henry's bedside, bathing the small body in an effort to keep him cool. She turned as Ellen rushed in. 'He seems a bit better. The rash has faded a little,' she said, smiling.

Ellen looked down at him. 'I was so worried,' she whispered.

'It is always hard with a first child — you don't know what to do and out here there is often no-one to ask for advice. So, they come to the doctor when sometimes there is no need.'

That explained her earlier attitude, Ellen thought. But it was surely not her place to decide who should see her employer.

The door opened and Richard came in, bringing that little jolt of the heart that the sight of him always gave her. He dismissed the housekeeper and came over to the bed where Henry now seemed to be sleeping more normally. He carried out his examination and gave a satisfied sigh. 'You can tell your husband that the baby is going to be all right. We'll keep him here just in case but it seems the fever has broken . . . '

'He's not my husband,' Ellen interrupted.

'Not . . . ?' Richard glanced down at her left hand. 'Oh, Ellen — I'm so sorry. But I don't understand. Your friends told me you were to be married and you said yourself you were engaged.'

'I'm not married, Patrick is my brother-in-law.'

Richard's face twisted with anger and he grabbed at her hand. She tried to pull away, angry herself now. What right did he have to judge her?

Before she could speak, his face changed. 'What about your fiancé? Did he make promises and then desert you? He should be made to . . . '

As Ellen realised his anger was not directed at her, her own temper softened. 'Richard, I am not married — and Henry is not my child,' she said quietly.

Her heart soared at the expression of relief and joy on his face. Did this mean that he returned her feelings? She allowed him to lead her to a chair and he sat opposite her, holding both her hands in his. 'Forgive me, Ellen. You must tell me the whole story — and how I could have been so mistaken. I've been a fool — and wasted a whole year into the bargain.'

It took a while to explain and Ellen's voice choked with tears when she came to relate her sister's death and her fears for the baby she had come to love as her own.

Richard leaned forward and took her

in his arms. 'Ellen, my darling, I can't bear to think how much you have suffered. And yet, you have coped so bravely.' He kissed her gently then drew back. 'Forgive me. I hope I do not presume too much? You have not yet told me what happened to the man you were to marry. Did he not return from the gold fields with your brother-in-law?'

Ellen didn't want to talk about James. She just wanted to stay in Richard's arms, and for him to go on kissing her. But she had to be honest with him. 'I have not formally released him from our engagement but I believe he has fallen in love with my friend, Joan. I only want them both to be happy.'

'And you, Ellen — would you be happy with that? You do not love him?'

Ellen looked into Richard's eyes. 'There is only one man I have ever loved — a man I thought I would never see again.' She gave a mischievous smile. 'Besides, I was not sure if he loved me.'

'Oh, Ellen, how could you doubt it? I

186

loved you from the moment I first saw you braving the wind and waves on board the ship. And getting to know you during that voyage only made me love you more.'

This time his kiss was far from gentle. The pressure of his lips on hers awoke in her a passion which she had never thought to experience. She responded with ardour until a small cry made them spring apart.

They rose and crossed the room to look down on little Henry who had awoken and now lay gazing round him with clear eyes. He was still flushed but the rash had died down and he was breathing normally.

Ellen turned to Richard, tears sparkling on her lashes. 'Thank God,' she whispered. 'And thank you, my love.'

His answer was to take her in his arms once more and, as Ellen felt his heart beating against hers, she felt that the voyage which had started so long ago was now truly over and she'd come to rest in a safe harbour.

Other titles in the
Linford Romance Library:

DEAR OBSESSION

I. M. Fresson

Dr. Manley's wife Kate has allowed her son Johnnie to become an obsession, excluding the rest of her family. However, when the doctor takes a new partner, Dr. Paul Quest, everything changes. Johnnie becomes more independent and her husband less willing to go along with her obsession. Kate, now realising that she is in danger of losing her husband, must also accept the bitter truth: that Johnnie is capable of doing without her . . .

ALL TO LOSE

Joyce Johnson

Katie Loveday decides to abandon
college to realise her dream of
transforming the family home into a
country house hotel and spa. With
the financial backing of her beloved
grandfather the business looks to be
a runaway success. But after a tragic
accident and the ensuing family
squabbles Katie fears she may have
to sell her hotel. When she also believes
the man she has fallen in love with
has designs on her business, the future
looks bleak indeed . . .

ERRAND OF LOVE

A. C. Watkins

Jancy Talliman flies halfway around the world to Bungalan, in Australia, to renew an interrupted love affair with Michael Rickwood, who she'd met in London. She remains undaunted on discovering that he's unofficially engaged to Cynthia Meddow, especially given the support of Michael's brother Quentin, and his sister Susan. Jancy settles in a small town nearby. Then as she becomes involved with the townspeople, dam worker Arnulf, and Quentin, Jancy alters the very reason for her long journey south . . .

A NEW BEGINNING

Toni Anders

Rowena had only met her godmother once, so why had Leonora Lawton left Cherry Cottage to her in her will? Should Rowena sell her bequest and continue to run her successful children's nursery, or make a new beginning in the chocolate box cottage two hundred miles away? The antagonism of Kavan Reagan, her attractive neighbour, who had hoped to inherit the cottage himself, only strengthens her resolve to make a new life for herself.

DAYS LIKE THESE

Miranda Barnes

Meg is devastated when her husband, the unreliable Jamie, leaves her. But life goes on. She develops a friendship with a colleague, Robert. Then Meg makes the bittersweet discovery that she is pregnant with Jamie's child. When Jamie reappears, she can't bring herself to tell him he is to be a father — until it's too late . . . Baby James arrives, and Meg resolves to be as good a parent as she possibly can. But it's Robert, not Jamie, she misses . . .

LOVE AT FIRST SIGHT

Chrissie Loveday

How could anyone not fall in love with Cameron? Handsome, rich, funny, caring — the sort of man every girl dreams of. And he had fallen in love with Megan. She couldn't say 'no' to his offer of marriage and she was swept along in a whirl of preparations. Was he just too good to be true? How well did she really know him? What was the old saying — 'marry in haste, repent at leisure'? She just hoped the second part wasn't true . . .